Harley wondered how she could *feel* someone so completely when she wasn't even touching that person.

"I have to go," Micah said. He walked to the door. Harley followed, ready to lock up when he left. She stayed a short distance behind him. She felt as if her flesh and blood, muscle and bone, had come alive, as if neurons or atoms or other chemical entities were flashing through her system with tiny sparks of red-hot fire. He had to leave, otherwise she'd embarrass herself.

But she didn't really care.

Still, he was right. They needed time. Just because they could hook up didn't mean they should forget that there were consequences to any deed, even if neither had any expectations.

At the door, he turned to her.

She walked forward, her eyes on his, until she was touching him, and when she did, he backed into the door. At the same time, his arms came around her.

She let herself touch his face. Stroke his cheek, feel the power in his arms as he drew her close. She shuddered with delicious abandon as she felt the heat of his body, the texture and strength in his muscles. And then she felt his mouth, crushing hers, and she returned the kiss with equal passion.

SHADOWS IN THE NIGHT

New York Times Bestselling Author

HEATHER GRAHAM

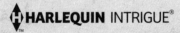

Recycling programs
for this product may
not exist in your area.

ISBN-13: 978-0-373-75709-1

Shadows in the Night

Printed in U.S.A.

New York Times and *USA TODAY* bestselling author **Heather Graham** has written more than a hundred novels. She's a winner of the RWA's Lifetime Achievement Award and the Thriller Writers' Silver Bullet. She is an active member of International Thriller Writers and Mystery Writers of America. For more information, check out her website, theoriginalheathergraham.com, or find Heather on Facebook.

Books by Heather Graham

Harlequin Intrigue

Law and Disorder
Shadows in the Night

MIRA Books

Wicked Deeds
Dark Rites
Dying Breath
A Perfect Obsession
Darkest Journey
Deadly Fate
Haunted Destiny
Flawless

Visit the Author Profile page at Harlequin.com for more titles.

CAST OF CHARACTERS

Harley Frasier—Criminology student on Tomlinson's expedition to find the tomb of the Ancient Egyptian ruler Amenmose.

Micah Fox—FBI special agent on leave from the DC office. Was once a student of Henry's.

Henry Tomlinson—Egyptologist, scholar, explorer, mentor.

Arlo Hampton—Young, eager Egyptologist with Alchemy.

Ned Richter—CEO of Alchemy, the private corporation sponsoring the expedition.

Vivian Richter—Eager Egyptologist and Ned's wife.

Belinda Gray—Egyptology student with a military fiancé in the Middle East.

Roger Eastman—Tech-oriented grad student.

Joe Rosello—Egyptology grad student and major flirt.

Jensen Morrow—Grad student in Egyptology, good-looking, hardworking, close to Harley.

Satima Mahmoud—Local interpreter.

Yolanda Akeem—Egyptian government liaison.

Gordon Vincent—Director, New Museum of Antiquity.

McGrady and Rydell—NYPD detectives.

Richard Egan—Supervising director, New York City office of the FBI.

Craig Frasier—Harley's cousin. FBI agent in the New York City office. Involved with Kieran.

Kieran Finnegan—Psychologist who consults for law enforcement. Co-owner of Finnegan's pub.

Dear Reader,

I'll never forget my "first" mummies. I think I was about five when we met.

My mom and her family immigrated here from Ireland when she was a teenager. She eventually married my dad, and while the two of them made the decision to move to Florida, my mom's family stayed in the Chicago area. That included my great-grandmother and a lot of wonderful crazy Irish family.

Naturally, we traveled from Florida to Chicago frequently when I was a child.

And thus—among other great institutions!—I was taken to the Field Museum of Natural History with a bunch of inventive storytellers. One example: Nefer-hoho (a made-up name, yes) had been a dancer and a jester, but she had danced too close to a brazier and it had hit her on the head and...next up, mummification. Then there was the mummified cat, who was magical, of course, and came alive in the museum at night. You had to be very careful to be out of the museum before dark, I was told, because the pharaoh would awaken and take his sword and...

As a five-year-old, I was (as an uncle explained to my mother) a wee bit traumatized by all these stories. Nightmares abounded!

But a lifelong fascination was born.

Years ago, my husband, Dennis, and I were able to visit Egypt, to see the Great Pyramid of Giza, the museum in Cairo and learn more about the culture.

This is a long and roundabout way of explaining that much of the Egyptology in this novel is true—but then again, I did spend those days with Irish storytellers, so some of what you're about to read is entirely made-up.

I could tell you which is which. But maybe you'll want to explore—or maybe you know far more than I ever will about the subject. Anyway, it's all part of a new story, and I sincerely hope you'll enjoy it.

If you'd like to comment on the story (I love to hear from readers!) or learn about upcoming books, contests, etc., please visit my website, theoriginalheathergraham.com. Thank you so much for being a reader!

Heather

Prologue

The Mummy
A Year Ago

"Sir!"

The word was spoken softly and with respect.

Dr. Henry Tomlinson, renowned Egyptologist, turned. One of the grad students had just slipped through the inner flap of the air-controlled prep tent and was smiling benignly, awaiting his attention.

He hadn't actually taught in about five years, but he still loved it—and working with students. He'd retired to spend all his time in the field, and he'd recently been hired by Alchemy, an Anglo-American sponsoring company, to head this dig. Alchemy was into all kinds of tech and had become a Fortune 500 company. Every year, they sponsored an ex-

ceptional archeological event, followed by a
public exhibit. Recent ones had been centered
around the Amazon River, central China—
and now ancient Egypt. Their resources were
phenomenal and Henry still couldn't believe
his good fortune. But no matter what monetary resources had been offered, he was
thrilled about having grad students involved.

This one was Harley Frasier. Just twenty-
six, she was tall, shapely, honey blonde, with
a face crafted in perfect classic symmetry and
enormous green eyes that seemed to take in
everything. She was serious and brilliant and
could nail the crux of information with laser-
like acuity. She also had a sense of humor and
the most delightful laugh he had ever heard.

Of the five specialty graduate candidates,
she was, beyond a doubt, his favorite. He often
felt like a grandfatherly mentor to her—and
the idea made him happy. He'd had no children of his own. He'd never even had a wife.
No time for a family. He hadn't intended it
be that way forever, but there was always so
much to do. If he'd had the chance to be a
father, he would've been pleased and proud
to have had Harley as a granddaughter. She
seemed to feel the same closeness to him.

Perhaps their bond was odd since, of the
five grad students, she was the one who was

different, the only one not majoring in Egyptology—though she was minoring in it. She had no plan to go into Egyptology or even archeology or history for her life's vocation.

Harley was with him, first of all, because of her knowledge regarding the field and her love for it. But she was also there because her work was going to be in criminal psychology and forensic science. Henry had been baffled when he was approached by her university. Professors at the Maryland college Harley was attending—which was arguably the top school for criminology and it also offered majors and minors in Egyptology and archeology—had explained to him the importance of having a student like Harley on this expedition. He had been on the hunt for the tomb of Amenmose for nearly a decade; for that entire decade, he'd been finding more and more clues about the location—and, of course, with the permission and blessing of the Egyptian government—finding other ancient tombs and treasures in the process. This allowed for his continued excavations. But the discovery of the tomb of Amenmose was the main focus of his work.

Many others had searched.

Some of them had died or disappeared in that effort.

History suggested that Amenmose had been

murdered. As a criminology student, Harley was to be in on the discovery and would seek and find whatever evidence those who had managed his secret burial might have left behind.

Not that, to Henry's mind, Amenmose hadn't deserved murder. He had usurped power every step of the way. He'd abused officials below him. It had even been intimated that he had attempted to kill those in power above him.

"I think we've gotten all the manual labor done for the evening and we're going to pack it in, maybe drive to that little town for some dinner. Want to come with us? You should. You'd enjoy it. Or shall we bring you back something?" Harley asked him.

"Next time, Harley, I'll come with you all," he promised. "There's so much in here! I'm not going to go touching anything until we've had a chance to work with the preservation measures, but I do intend to look at everything."

Earlier that week, they had finally discovered the secret site of the tomb of Amenmose. And, of course, since then, Henry Tomlinson had been on cloud nine. This was a dream come true, a fantasy realized, the culmination of a lifetime of love and dedication.

Harley laughed softly. "Yes! You did it, Dr. Tomlinson."

"I did, didn't I?"

The Amenmose find was among the most important ancient Egyptian discoveries of the past few years; he couldn't have been more excited about being a major player in that discovery. And even now, at the end of an exhausting day—and even though he truly enjoyed the young people working with him—he was far too fascinated to leave. There were a dozen or so coffins to be studied, one of them presumably that of Amenmose; the group wouldn't consider opening them until everyone was back at the museum in Cairo. But he *could* study the canopic jars they'd found thus far. There were also other artifacts that had been carefully moved into the prep tent. So much to observe and to describe! And there were the broken coffins, which had probably been as meticulously set as any of the others, but had been in the section where a partial cave-in had taken place. Several of those outer and inner coffins had split and exposed their mummies. Henry Tomlinson was fascinated to see what study was possible before the mummies were packed and crated and prepared for the trip to Cairo, where options for preservation were far more sophisticated, and where the mummies could be X-rayed and DNA could be tested.

Oh! It was all so monumental.

Amenmose had been a priest in the days when another priest, Ay, had ruled Egypt as regent. Ay had done so for a well-known pharaoh, the boy king, Tutankhamen. As regent, Ay had wielded immense power. He'd gone on to become pharaoh in his own right—after the death of Tut at the age of nineteen.

Amenmose, according to ancient texts, had tried to usurp some of that power. And he'd had his own followers in the court, making him a dangerous man. Because of this he had feared for his immortal life—and his wife had kept his burial plans a complete secret, shared only with members of his family. Naturally, legend had it that many of his most loyal followers—rather than give away any secrets—had been willing to die with him, sealed alive in a grave for eternity.

"Dr. Tomlinson, you worked so hard. And wow! You triumphed. You should celebrate. Come out with us. Is there nothing I can do to convince you?" Harley asked. She still had that wonderful smile, as if she were the one who was far older and wiser. "Nothing's going to disappear. We'll go have some dinner and drinks and come on back. There are plenty of men on guard here. And," she added, "you really deserve a little celebration with us. Think of it—you researched and imagined and looked into the ancient Egyptian mind and you made the discovery. It's your shining moment. You're another Carter with his Tutankhamen, Dr. Tomlinson. Do you realize that?"

"Oh, no, no," Henry demurred. He shook his head firmly. "A celebration is tempting, but I couldn't leave. I couldn't. I do promise that I'll come with all of you on another day. Harley! Look at this! I feel like, as the song says, I have treasures untold."

Harley laughed. "You saw *The Little Mermaid*?" she asked.

He stared at her, feeling a bit chagrined. "Oh! Yes, I get it, you wouldn't think that I'd see a children's movie…" He laughed, too. "Remember, I do have great nieces and nephews! Anyway…"

He started walking as he spoke. "Harley, these are such treasures! This broken coffin." He gestured at it. "Damaged by time and by that cave-in, however many centuries ago. And this fellow, Harley. It almost looks as if he was buried alive. Wrapped up alive and screaming."

"I don't think you can embalm anyone

and have that person come out of the process alive," Harley reminded him, amused. "That's only in fiction. We both know what was involved in Egyptian embalming, and just how many factors could've had an effect on the mummy's appearance. Screaming mummies belong to B movies, right? And when you think about it, weird mummies are all the more reason you should come with us."

"Why is that?"

Harley didn't answer. The flap opened again and Jensen Morrow, another of the students, poked his head in to answer.

He'd obviously heard the question.

"Ooh! 'Cause you shouldn't be alone with scary old stuff when you have cool kids like us to hang out with!" Jensen said.

They all laughed. Jensen was a good-looking, dark-haired young man who loved the study he was involved in, and Dr. Henry Tomlinson liked him very much, as well. Jensen played hard, but he worked harder. He came from money; his father was an inventor who'd come up with a special cleaning product. And yet Jensen never acted like money, never acted pretentious or entitled the way some rich kids did.

"Tempting, tempting, tempting," Henry said again. "But I'm going to stay."

Jensen raised his eyebrows at Harley. "Hey, girl, then it's you and me heading out. The old man here isn't coming. That's okay. We're bringing back the goods. Just the two of us, since Belinda Gray is waiting for a video chat with her fiancé—military, as we know!—in Iraq. Roger Eastman agreed to help one of the tech guys investigate some computer info they're picking up. I hate to say it, but we're getting chatter about an insurgent group starting up. And Joe Rosello said he wants to learn more about the excavation equipment. He's working with that pretty Egyptian girl, our translator, and learning about hoists."

"Hoists? Yeah, right!" Harley said. "Satima. She *is* pretty, and thank goodness we have her. I'm just grateful she filled in at the last minute when the older gentleman we'd hired wound up ill. If I know our friend Joe at all, I know he's very happy!" she said to Henry. "We won't go far, since we seem to be feeling a wee bit nervous! And we won't be late. We'll bring you something to eat and see if you want to be social when we get back, okay? If, and only if, you're absolutely positive you don't want to take a ride with this handsome, if ridiculous, guy and me?"

Henry laughed. "Oh, Harley, you're a sweetheart, but give it up. You know I'm not coming."

She grimaced, a delightful movement of her face. "Yes, I do," she admitted. "But we— your devoted students—have to try. I'll bring you a special treat for dinner."

"Don't worry about me, guys. I'll be fine."

"Sorry, we *will* worry about you. At least we can make sure you eat. I'm willing to bet you're going to be up all night—and you won't even notice that you haven't slept," Harley said.

He smiled and made a shooing motion with his hands. "Go! Get on out with you. Be young and have fun and don't become an obsessive old curmudgeon like me. Jensen, get her out of here!"

"Yes, sir!" Jensen said.

Harley still hung back. "You're neither obsessive nor old," she insisted. "Okay, wait. Maybe you are obsessive. Anyway, we'll be back by nine or so, and like I said, I'll bring you something delicious."

"Sounds lovely! See you soon."

And at last, Harley and Jensen left.

Dr. Henry Tomlinson turned his attention back to Unknown Mummy #1 for several long moments. Many pharaohs and royalty and even esteemed but lesser men, like Amenmose, ended up with unknowns in their tombs—servants needed in the next life.

Almost the entire lid of the coffin had been torn open. That afternoon, two of the students had painstakingly cleared out the rubble around the mummy. But Henry felt as if he was indeed looking at remnants featured in a B horror flick; the thing really did appear to be a man who'd been wrapped up with his mouth open in horror, left to silently scream into eternity.

Mummies weren't wrapped like this alive. Unless, of course...

He'd never been intended to be a mummy?

He'd been a murder victim.

Could this unidentified mummy be Amenmose himself? he wondered excitedly. They hadn't identified the man's tomb.

Great question, but it wasn't scientific to jump to conclusions. X-rays would give them an image of the insides—and that would probably tell them if the facial contortions had happened because of some accident in the drying process or if he *had* somehow been wrapped alive!

No, it couldn't be Amenmose, Henry decided. According to the ancient texts and all the information at his disposal, Amenmose had died before burial. Besides, they'd discovered one coffin in an inner tomb, deep in a hidden recess—again, just as the ancient texts had said. Amenmose's enemies might have defiled his tomb if those who loved him hadn't concealed his remains. The mummy here, found in the outer chamber, couldn't be Amenmose—not unless there was a great deal they were missing! "Sorry, old boy. Lord only knows what happened to you," Henry told the mummy.

"Hey!"

The inner flap to the preparation tent opened again. Henry looked over to see that it was Alchemy's director at large, Ned Richter.

He was smiling. As he should have been. Their day had been fantastic.

"Hey," Henry said. He liked Richter okay. Although not an Egyptologist himself, the man was studious and yet always ready help out with manual labor when needed.

Henry didn't like Richter's wife, Vivian, so much. She was an Egyptologist, too—at least in her own mind, he thought with a snort. Okay, so she did have her master's degree from Brown; she was just annoying as hell and she didn't think clearly or reason anything out. She was an attractive enough woman with short dark hair and dark eyes, and she claimed the maternal side of her father's family had been Egyptian.

She liked to pretend that she knew what she was talking about.

She seldom did.

"Just checking on you!" Richter said.

Henry heard Vivian speaking behind her husband. "Tell him to come with us. We'll get some food and drinks."

"Hey, Viv!" Henry called out. "I'm good tonight. Going to work. And a couple of the students are picking me up something to eat. Listen," he added in a more affable voice, "can't wait till you and I have a chance to talk tomorrow. We can compare notes then!"

"Can't you make him come?" Henry heard Vivian whisper.

"No," Richter said flatly. "He's head of the examination and prep all the way through the removal to Cairo—by Alchemy and the Egyptian government. As you know," he muttered.

"See you in the morning!" Henry called pleasantly. Yes!

But he'd barely turned around before he heard the inner tent flap opening again.

This time, it was Arlo Hampton, the Egyptologist who'd been employed specifically by Alchemy to watch over their investment.

Arlo was young—tall, straight and a little skinny. He preferred his thick glasses to contact lenses. Good thing for Arlo that nerds were in; he was, beyond a doubt, a nerd. But a friendly and outgoing nerd. He loved Egyptology, and yet, unlike certain other people, he wasn't full of himself or convinced that he knew everything.

"Hey, I knew you'd be alone with the treasures, snug as a bug in a rug!" Arlo told him cheerfully. There was something slightly guilty in his voice. "I wanted to make sure you were okay, though."

"I'm great. And, of course, if you want to join me..."

"I'm beat, Henry. I'm what? Thirty years younger than you? I don't know how you do it. I'm going to have a sandwich with the grad students when Harley and Jensen get back, and then hit my bunk until tomorrow. If that's okay. I mean, I should be like you, hard at work... Oh, I did just meet Belinda's boyfriend on Skype. Seems like a decent guy. So Belinda, Roger and Joe are taking care of their personal business, and then we're all going to meet and after that—"

"I saw Harley and Jensen. They'll bring me food. You're fine, Arlo. Have a nice night."

"Yeah, thanks. Strange, though. Something doesn't feel right his evening. Am I just being paranoid?"

"Yes. And shoo. Go on, Arlo. You worked

He shook his head, impatient with himself. He was incredibly lucky to have this time alone in the preparation tent. He'd been the one to do the research and the calculations; he'd been the one who'd garnered the sponsorship that had provided the money for this expedition. His papers had raised significant interest. It was—yes, indeed—his baby.

But eventually Dr. Arlo Hampton would want his time here, his chance to study these mummies, these treasures. So would Yolanda Akeem, their liaison with the Department of Antiquities. Then, of course, there was Ned Richter...and his wife. He'd bet that Richter couldn't care less if he got any time with the mummies and ancient treasures or not. Richter was there to guard Alchemy's interests and, Henry suspected, to ensure that they looked as if they were being incredibly magnanimous to the Egyptian government. After all, Alchemy financed these expeditions, he was almost certain, for tax breaks—and the media attention and promotion they provided.

Fine. The excavation was a great success. And this was *his* time. His time alone with all his treasures!

He started to go back to his work, but he

could've sworn he'd seen movement from the corner of his eye.

He stood up and walked around.

Nothing.

Henry sat back down and continued his recording.

"Ancient Egypt—"

There *was* something behind him!

He tried to spin about.

And he saw nothing but binding, the linen binding that had been used on the ancient dead, saw it wrapped around fingers and a hand, saw the fingers and the hand circle his neck and—

Fingers, like wire, clutching his throat, so powerful, so strong...

He fought their hold. Wriggled and squirmed. He tried to rise; he couldn't. The pain was terrible. The world began to blacken before him; little dots of light exploded in the darkness. And all he could think was that—

The mummy!

The mummy had risen to kill him!

It was impossible. Impossible. Impossible...

He was a scientist. Rational. He didn't believe.

He was a scientist...

And as the last electrons exploded against

the stygian pit of his dying mind, he couldn't help but think…

He was a scientist.

Being killed by an ancient Egyptian mummy.

It didn't make sense. It wasn't right.

Chapter One

One Year Later
The New Museum of Antiquity
New York City, New York

The moon that shone down through the sky-lights in the temple region of the museum created a stunning vision. Opalescent light shimmered on the marble and made it appear that the ribbon of "Nile" river by the temple was created of crystal and glass. The lights in the area were dim, designed to look as if they were burning torches set along the walls.

The exhibit in the New Museum of Antiquity was impressive—even to Harley, despite all the time she'd spent in the real Sahara. In designing this space, the organizers had also borrowed heavily from another famous NYC museum, all to the benefit of the Egyptian displays. Harley felt a sudden breeze from an air-conditioning vent, and she shivered.

"Mummy thing getting to you, huh?"

"Pardon?" Harley turned quickly to see the speaker. The words had been teasing; they'd also been spoken in a pleasantly deep, masculine voice.

The voice aroused a strange memory she couldn't quite reach—and seemed to whisper to something inside her, far beneath her skin.

She hadn't seen the speaker before, despite the fact that his voice seemed oddly familiar. Here, on opening night, she should've known most of the invited crowd. But she didn't know him, and—as her chosen field of criminology had taught her—she studied anyone she didn't recognize in a situation such as this evening's event.

A soiree to celebrate the exhibition. This was opening night for the traveling exhibit that would, in the end, return to Egypt, where the precious artifacts of that country would then remain. But tonight they celebrated the very first time the exhibit had been seen! It would open to the public in the morning. It had, quite properly, been named in honor of Henry—the Henry Tomlinson Collection of Egyptian Culture and Art.

There would be toasts in his honor, of course.

This phenomenal display would not have been possible without him.

But Henry was gone, as much a part of history as his treasures.

She sensed that this man—with his deep, somehow familiar voice—was connected to Henry.

She definitely hadn't seen him before.

He wasn't the kind of man you forgot.

He was tall—well over six feet, she thought. Because she'd recently taken identification classes that taught criminologists to look for details to include in descriptions, she also noted that not only was he about six foot three, but he had excellent posture. Nicely muscled, too. She had no doubt that he was the kind of man who spent time in a gym, not to create impressive abs, but to train the complex human machine that was his most important tool.

How could she be so sure of this? she asked herself. And yet she was.

He wore a casual suit, no jewelry. He was freshly shaven, and kept his dark hair cropped close to his head.

Someone's bodyguard?

Beneath the glimmer of the moon that showed through the skylights, she couldn't quite ascertain the color of his eyes. She had a feeling they were light, despite the darkness of his hair.

Thirty-three to thirty-six years old, she estimated. Carefully nondescript clothing—dark blue suit, dark blue shirt, pin-striped tie in shades of blue and black. Sunglasses resting on head.

He moved closer to her; she was certain he'd been doing the same kind of study on her that she'd nearly completed on him.

No, she'd never seen him before, but she *had* heard his voice.

"Sorry. I didn't mean to interrupt. You're not afraid of mummies, right?" he asked again, his expression quizzical.

"No, not at all," she assured him. "Ah, well, that's a bit of a lie. I might be afraid of some of the bacteria that can be found in old tombs, but as for the mummies themselves...no. My dad was a cop, a very good one. He taught me to fear the living, not the dead."

"Sounds like a bright man," he said. He stepped toward her, offering his hand. "Micah. Micah Fox."

She shook his hand. "Harley Frasier. How do you do? And pardon me, but who are you? Do I know you?"

He smiled. "Yes, and no. I'm an old student of Dr. Tomlinson's," he said. "I was at

Brown when he was teaching there. About twelve years ago, I was lucky enough to join him on one of his expeditions. Back then, he was looking for the tomb of a princess from the Old Kingdom, Fifth Dynasty." He paused, still smiling, and shrugged. "He found her, too—right now she's in one of the display cases in a room not far from here, near the temple." He stopped, studying her again, and asked, "Are you surprised by that?"

"No, no, I'm not. You don't look like an Egyptologist," Harley said. "Sorry! It's not that Egyptologists look a certain way. I just—"

"It's okay. I'm not an Egyptologist," he told her. "I meant is it surprising that he found his princess? No, of course not. Henry was the best. But even though I began in archeology, I changed my major. I'm with the government now."

"FBI?" Harley guessed.

He nodded.

"Something seems to be coming back. I'm not sure what," she said. "I know your voice, but I don't know *you*. I mean—"

"Yes, you know my voice. I guess I should start over. I called you soon after the incident when you were staying in Rome. Your group was shipped from place to place, and we were trying to get a handle on what happened. I'm the Fox from those phone calls. Special Agent Micah Fox—though I admit, I was working on my own, and not as assigned by the bureau. And I apologize, because I do know a lot about you, although it wasn't appropriate to bring that up at the time. You're Craig Frasier's first cousin, and Craig and I have actually worked together. Of course, we're in different offices now. Naturally, you've met a number of the men and women with the New York office. Craig told me you finished grad school, and you're deciding what to do with all your education—join up with NYPD's finest, remain with the private agency employing you now, or go into a federal agency. But tonight, you're here for the same reason I am, honoring our old professor. For one summer, you were an unofficial Egyptologist. And, as I just explained, you recognize my voice because we spoke on the phone. I'm Criminal Division, FBI. Right now, I'm assigned down in DC. I've taken some leave to be here."

"I…see," she said.

Did she?

No, not really.

Wait. Fox—yes, that was the name of the man she'd spoken with about Henry Tomlinson, just once, what now seemed like a lifetime ago.

These days, that time was mostly a blur. Maybe because she didn't *want* to think of it. But she couldn't stop her mind from rushing back to the night they'd returned to the camp, laughing and loaded down with food and drink for their professor, only to find him on the floor, along with the broken coffin and the "screaming" mummy. He'd been garroted by his own belt, eyes open and bulging, throat blackened and bruised, a swatch of ancient linen wrapped around it.

There'd been an immediate outcry. Security was convinced that no one from outside had been anywhere near the expedition tents; they kept a tight perimeter around the work area, which included the tents that had been set up for the staff. Egyptian police had come out, ready to help with the investigation.

Then, all hell had broken loose. The computer had picked up more chatter. And word had come that the fledgling, unaffiliated militant group calling themselves The Ancient Guard was bearing down on the expedition. Perhaps they intended to steal the artifacts to finance their cause. Not an uncommon scenario... It meant that everyone and everything needed to go as quickly as possible. Government forces were being sent out, but no one wanted scientists from around the world caught up in an exchange of gunfire.

Security forces from Alchemy, along with the Egyptian police, did their best to preserve what they could from the expedition, as well as the body of Henry Tomlinson so they could discover the circumstances of his death.

Much was lost. But at least no one else was killed. The final inquiry, conducted by the Egyptian police and the Alchemy security force, concluded that the brilliant archeologist Dr. Henry Tomlinson had driven himself mad and committed suicide. According to their conclusions, he believed a mummy had come to life with the intention of murdering him… It was suspected that some unknown bacteria had caused the temporary fit of insanity, and everything from the expedition would be scrutinized using proper precautions.

Harley had fought the verdict—vociferously. She was a criminology student; she knew what should have been done and a lot of it wasn't. Pretty much nothing had been done, really, not as far as a crime scene examination went.

Not in her opinion, anyway.

How many men committed suicide with

their own belts in such a manner? She sure as hell hadn't seen or read about any. And she was *studying* criminology.

Nope, never heard of it!

Her friends backed her up, at first. And then, one by one, it seemed, they all decided that the poor professor—so caught up in his love and enthusiasm for his work—had gone mad, even if only temporarily. No one could find a motive for murdering him. Henry Tomlinson had been respected and dearly loved by everyone. No one could find a clue.

The police assigned to them had been incompetent, to Harley's mind. Authorities in Egypt and in the United States hadn't done enough.

And the Alchemy people…

They wanted it to be a suicide. They didn't want to deal with a murder. They accepted the verdict without a whimper.

They were so sorry and sad, they'd claimed, and in hindsight, they could see so many mistakes.

They should've known to be more careful!

Henry should've known to be more careful!

But in fact, they said, the professor's enthusiasm for the project had caused them all to bypass modern safety regulations that might have kept him alive.

A great company line, Harley thought in disgust.

And what was the matter with her? They might all have been killed by a crazy insurgent group that hadn't defined exactly what it was fighting for or against. It was a miracle that they'd gotten out, that they were all alive.

Well, most of them. And Henry, poor Henry, he'd done himself in—according to the authorities and to Alchemy, who went on to say that now they'd never completely understand the biology of what had gone on. They weren't allowed back on the site; the Egyptian government had stamped a foot down hard.

And that night…

First, they were shuffled to Cairo, then, almost immediately—on the orders of the Egyptian authorities and the US State Department—they were put on planes to Rome, and from Rome they were flown to New York City.

But, thinking back, Harley recalled that it was while she'd been staying at the little Italian hotel near the Spanish Steps that she'd spoken with this man. Fox. He'd wanted to know whatever she knew about the situation, and she'd told him everything, adding that she didn't believe a word of the official explanation.

There was no way Henry had killed himself.

Special Agent Fox had seemed to accept her version, but apparently he'd been just as stonewalled as she had.

Like her, he'd been forced to realize in the end that no one was going to believe him. Or her.

And even if the authorities had believed him, they didn't care enough to make a killer pay!

Here, tonight, for the first time in a year, everything about that horrible occasion was suddenly coming back.

Tonight was about honoring Henry Tomlinson. This would be an event during which people would shake their heads sadly, missing the professor who'd done so much, declaring it tragic that he'd lost his mind because of what he'd loved so deeply.

"Ms. Frasier?"

She blinked, staring at the man in front of her, wondering how long she'd been lost in her own thoughts.

In a way, she did know him. They'd just never met in person. She'd left the Sahara before he reached it. Then she'd been flown out of Cairo, and soon after that she was back in New York.

"I'm sorry!" she said softly.

He shook his head. "Hey, it's all right. I know you really cared, and that you tried to do something. It must have been hard to maintain your own belief that he'd been murdered when everyone else was telling you otherwise," Micah Fox said.

It had been and still was. "Oh, don't you know?" she muttered. "'Henry went crazy. Bacteria in the wrappings. He just *had* to dig in before proper precautions were taken. It's so tragic—don't make it worse by rehashing every little thing!'"

Her tone, she knew, was heavy with sarcasm.

They were alone in the temple area—or so she believed. Still, she looked around and repeated, "I'm sorry. I tried... I do believe he was murdered. They did find bacteria, but not enough. Henry was murdered. And I couldn't do a damned thing to prove it."

Micah nodded at her. She liked his face. Hard-jawed, somewhat sharp-boned. His eyes, she saw now, were actually blue—sky blue—and they seemed to see a great deal.

"Remember, I was a student of his, too. And

now I'm an FBI agent. And I couldn't do anything, either. You have nothing to be sorry for." He paused. "I should explain. I knew about you through Craig, of course. And also through Henry. We kept in touch when we could—he'd let me know what was up, what was going on. I went into law enforcement, but I still love Egyptology. Henry thought the world of you." He shook his head. "I can only imagine what it was like that last night. I hope you're okay now. Time…heals, so they say."

"So they say."

"It heals when you're at peace with the past."

"And I'm not," she said grimly, and added, "And neither are you."

"No. Anyway, I'd like to find out about the last time you saw him. If you don't mind."

"There won't be a chance tonight," she said.

"I know. At a later date."

Harley nodded. "I'll be happy to speak with you. I'm not sure what I can tell you, though."

"You found him."

"Yes."

"I'd just like you to go over it with me. I realize it's painful, but…"

"The verdict was ridiculous! You know what the ME said! That he killed himself."

"An Egyptian ME, who wanted out of there

as quickly as possible, with armed insurrectionists about to attack the place."

True!

But then...

"The company, Alchemy, brought in a medical examiner, too. He agreed with the Egyptian ME's findings."

"I'm sure that all happened in about two
minutes in Cairo or Rome. And as soon as
they made their decision, Henry was shot
through with preservatives and packed into a
box. So anything that could be construed as
evidence was compromised. I could be way
off base. *We* could be way off base. Thing is,
I'd feel better if we could talk."

"Yes, of course," she said.

Of course?

She didn't want to remember that night!

And yet, here was someone—someone in
law enforcement—who agreed with her, the
only person who did. Like her, Fox believed
there was a truth out there that everyone else
had denied.

They looked at each other awkwardly for
a moment.

"Well, a pleasure to meet you in person.
I guess I'm going to head over to the party
area," Micah said. His voice softened. "I didn't
mean to interrupt you. You might want more

time here. On your own. By the way, as I said, I really do know your cousin fairly well. We worked together years ago on a case in DC. He's a great guy."

"Yes. Craig's great," Harley agreed.

She sensed that he wanted to say more.

Like maybe when or where they could meet again?

But he didn't speak. They weren't alone anymore.

Jensen Morrow came striding through the temple area. He apparently saw Harley, but not Micah Fox, probably because he stood in the shadow of a carved obelisk.

"I knew I'd find you here!" Jensen told Harley, heading toward her for a huge hug.

He'd written his thesis, gotten his graduate degree and taken a job here as an assistant curator, making use of his doctorate in Egyptology. He'd been her friend through her suspicions, her anger, her demands—and her final defeat, when she'd realized that nothing was going to be done.

No one was ever going to make her believe that Henry Tomlinson had been convinced that a mummy was attacking him—while strangling himself with his own belt.

Jensen, she was certain, had just given up.

He'd been told the lie so many times that to him, it had become truth.

Harley accepted Jensen's hug; she still cared about him. When they'd first met, they'd hit it off as friends. They might have become more at one time; he was fun, energetic and thoughtful, not to mention tall, dark and handsome. But everything had changed the night Henry Tomlinson died.

Even though she didn't see the friends she'd made in Egypt very often—they were all busy working, getting on with their lives—they had all stayed friends. They were, in fact, oddly close; they had shared the experience of the dig, Henry Tomlinson's death and the escape from the desert under dire circumstances in the middle of the night. All of that meant they had an emotional bond few people shared.

And yet it was a closeness stained with the loss of the man they'd all adored. Stained, too, by the way they'd fled on the very night he died, swept up in a reign of terror.

She'd gone on to finish her own graduate work, head bent to her studies, and had taken part-time work with a prestigious investigation firm in the city so that she could still take classes when she chose while deciding what path to take for her future. It felt right, for the time being. But she had to make some real decisions soon. And yet, even as she'd worked toward her educational and career goals, she had felt that she was waiting. A temporary post—with flexible hours!—was all she'd been willing to accept at the moment.

"They're about to start," Jensen said, pulling away from her to study her face. That was when he rather awkwardly noticed there was someone else in the temple exhibit.

He offered Micah Fox a hand. "I'm sorry. How rude. I didn't see you. I'm Jensen Morrow."

"Micah Fox," the other man returned. "And actually, we've spoken. Over the phone."

"Oh! Hey, that was you?" Jensen said. "Wow. Was I vague when I talked to you? Or worse, rude? If I was, I didn't mean to be. It's just that...well, you had to be there that night. We found Henry—or, I should say, Harley found Henry—and by the time the medical examiner arrived, they were screaming that the insurgents were a few miles out and we had to break camp ASAP! I know Harley and I were going crazy with concern and disbelief and...well...hey," he finished lamely.

"There wasn't anything you could have done to change the situation," Micah said.

"Well, you're FBI, right? I guess if you couldn't prove anything different from what was said or get anything done, Harley and I, who had no law enforcement power, couldn't have done more than complain and question. Which we did. Who knows? The thing is— thing that got me, anyway—we weren't in a closed or confined space. I mean if bacteria were going to get him, you might've thought someone else would've had a reaction or... Anyway, had you been assigned to the case— officially? The FBI works in Egypt? Or does it?"

"The FBI works all over the world, as necessary," Micah replied. "But... I was there because of Henry."

"Special Agent Fox was another of Henry's grad students, but years ago," Harley quickly explained.

"Ah," Jensen murmured. That was obviously enough of an explanation. "I guess you were crazy about him, too."

"I was. Brilliant man. Horrible circumstances."

Jensen glanced at Harley. "I think we were the last people who saw him. Alive, I mean. Harley was trying to get him to come out with us. But you knew him. There was no way he was going to leave his work that night."

"No, Henry wouldn't want to leave his

work." He paused, clearing his throat. "Well, I think they must be about ready to start."

"Let's go." Harley slid her fingers into Jensen's and they left, nodding to Micah. It was ludicrous, but she was suddenly afraid to be too close to the man. He not only projected strength—he was someone warm when the world had been cold. Too confident, too attractive...

She could easily give in to her feelings of sadness and loss and even anger on a night like this. With a man like this.

She was aware of Micah watching them leave.

And she wondered what he was thinking.

HARLEY FRASIER, CRAIG'S COUSIN, was certainly a beautiful young woman, Micah thought, watching her leave, hand in hand with Jensen Morrow. He'd been studying her intently for some time before he'd spoken with her. It was evident that she had really cared about Henry. And he knew how Henry had felt about her.

According to Craig, she had wonderful parents and a great older brother, living grandparents, all kinds of family life. Micah's parents had been lost in a bridge accident when he was a child; his aunt had raised him. Auntie

Jane. He loved her and she was a talented and compassionate woman. But she was it as far as family went. He had no siblings, no cousins— no one else anywhere that he knew about. His family went far back in Virginia history; it had simply winnowed down to him and Jane.

His father had been FBI. People had feared the dangers of his job. They'd never imagined that he might die young because of a bridge collapse.

Henry Tomlinson had treated him like a son or grandson. He'd shared his enthusiasm for Egyptology with Micah. Henry had a family he adored. He hadn't married, but he had a loving niece and nephew-in-law, and he was crazy about their kids.

He'd send Micah pictures of an unusual canopic jar right alongside ones of the kids with their new puppy. That was Henry.

Micah followed the pair who'd just left, wondering if he was indulging himself in an exercise of futility. Was the truth about Henry Tomlinson's death ever going to be uncovered? Henry had been murdered, which was terrible enough, but it had happened on a night when both the Egyptian government and the US Department of State had been determined to get all the workers away from the site and out of the country. The group who'd planned the attack had called themselves The Ancient Guard.

Apparently, they hadn't believed that Alchemy intended that the treasures they'd found would merely go on loan to the United States and other countries—and that they'd remain Egyptian property. Maybe they hadn't cared. And maybe, like most militant groups, what The Ancient Guard wanted, religious and political ideology aside, was a chance to fight and stave off frustration. And probably steal the treasures to finance their fighting.

They'd either been beaten back or dissipated quickly when met with armed resistance.

Micah had gone to Cairo to investigate Henry's death on an unofficial basis, and then to Rome, where the Alchemy crew had briefly stayed. Their communication had been by phone—he'd been a day behind each time everyone had moved on. And by the time he'd reached the States, it had all been too long.

Henry had been cremated, just as he'd instructed his niece to arrange in the event of his death. Then, of course, it was too late to bring in any experts.

But Henry had never suspected that he might be murdered.

And why would he?

Why the hell kill an academic like Henry?

The man had never wanted or kept anything for himself—he'd never tried to slip away with even the smallest, most insignificant artifact. His work had always been about sharing treasures with the world.

Tonight… Well, tonight, Micah could watch. He could see the people who'd been close to Henry in his last days.

The grand foyer of the museum had been chosen for the site of the private gala opening. The center monument here was a massive replica of a temple from Mesopotamia that sat in the center of a skylit rotunda. The museum was beautiful, and just down the street from its larger cousin, the Metropolitan. Many design ideas that worked well in the first had been used in this newer museum. The offices were deep in the basement, for the most part. The museum was dedicated to the ancient world; it was divided into sections that concentrated on the earliest humans to the rich, ancient civilizations of Greece, Egypt, Persia, Mesopotamia and more.

The exhibition hall that would open to the public in the morning was an admirable addition to the museum. Exhibits didn't stay forever, but the hall itself would continue to thrive because of the work of Henry and other archeologists and scholars; right now, however, it was all about Henry.

Men and women in pairs and groups stood around the room, chatting, while waiters and waitresses in white-and-black attire moved about with trays of hors d'oeuvres and flutes of champagne.

Many of those invited were here because they were sponsoring patrons of the museum. There were also a number of politicians, including the mayor.

None of them interested Micah.

He scanned the crowd, taking note of those he did find intriguing.

Arlo Hampton, young, pleasant, eager. Tall and slim, but handsomely boyish-looking in a suit, speaking with an Egyptian dignitary. Ned Richter and his wife, Vivian. He so robust, she so tiny, both smiling, standing close, chatting with the mayor. And there—between an aging Broadway director and his latest ingénue—Belinda Gray, sans her fiancé, who was still serving in the military. He saw Roger Eastman, wiry and lean, wearing thick-lensed glasses, talking with his hands as he loudly discussed a technical innovation for dealing with the security of priceless historic objects. Across the room, in the midst of a few young female museum apprentices, was Joe Rosello.

Joe seemed electrically energetic; he was a square-shouldered guy who could've been a fullback. He had a full head of curly dark hair and a very white smile.

Micah had done research on everyone involved with the last stages of the dig. Every one of the workers who'd had access to the tent. It hadn't been easy finding out about the Egyptian workers. Since they weren't archeologists or preservation experts, they hadn't been allowed into the inner sanctum of the camp, where the preparation tent was located. Still, he'd done his best. But everything in him screamed that the guilty party was not Egyptian, but someone among those who should have loved and honored Henry.

Why? he asked himself again. Why the hell would anyone kill Henry? If he could come up with a *why...*

"Micah?"

He turned. He hadn't expected to know many people here tonight. His name had been softly voiced by one of the few people he did know, and he knew her fairly well.

Simone Bixby, Henry Tomlinson's niece.

Simone was in her midthirties, a sandy-haired woman who looked eternally like a girl. She was small and slim and wide-eyed.

She was accompanied by her husband, Jerry, a banker, who was equally slim and wide-eyed.

Micah greeted them both.

"Thank you for coming. And thank you for caring so much," Simone said. "It's still so hard to accept what they say."

"Yes, it is," Micah agreed.

"But tonight," Jerry said brightly, "tonight we honor his body of work."

"Yes. An incredible body of work," Micah said. "How are the girls?"

"Getting big!" Simone answered. "Ten, eight and five now."

He nodded. "I've seen pictures. They're beautiful."

"They are. Thank you. They loved their uncle Henry, too," Simone said.

"We all miss him."

"Oh, look—there's Arlo Hampton," Jerry said. "Micah, we'll talk later? Simone, we need to find out what he wants us to do when he speaks."

"Excuse us," Simone said.

"Of course!" Micah told them. They moved on.

He continued to survey the room.

Hail, hail, the gang's all here. Grad students. Administration staff. Egyptologists. City officials. Museum people. And there…

An exotic woman with dark skin and almost inky black hair was speaking with Simone and her family. Arlo stood beside them.

Yolanda Akeem. They'd met briefly—very briefly—in Cairo. She was the Egyptian liaison with the Department of Antiquities. Naturally, she'd be here tonight.

She saw him looking at her. She elegantly lifted her glass a few inches in acknowledgment.

She'd given him whatever information she'd had in Cairo; it hadn't been much. A two-second autopsy report and a lecture on the dangers of the Middle East. He didn't listen to much of it. Henry's body was gone by then and the members of the expedition had been shuttled off. He'd been ready to follow them as quickly as possible when they'd been in Egypt—and through their escape from the trouble that had befallen the expedition that night.

Tonight, they were all here.

And there was Harley Frasier. She had a smile on her face as she spoke with Gordon Vincent, director at large for the museum. Her smile was forced. Jensen was with her, smiling and chatting, as well. He seemed to be putting a little too much effort into being charming.

Which didn't seem necessary, since he was already employed by the museum.

Harley didn't; she worked for Fillmore Investigations, a large security and investigation company that served the civilian market, but was known for its close affiliation with the New York City PD and other law enforcement agencies. The founder of the company, Edward Fillmore, had barely survived a kidnap-for-ransom scheme as a child. He had founded his company on the premise that all agencies, public or private, should work together for the benefit of victims. Since Micah's job with the FBI had come about because of similar circumstances, he liked the man without even knowing him. Micah was pleased that Harley Frasier had chosen such a reputable company. None of his business, of course. But...

He'd felt something for her, just from hearing her voice over the phone a year ago.

And now...he'd seen her.

Anyone awake and breathing would find her attractive and charming.

He was certainly charmed by her and impressed by her—and so much more.

Even though he hardly knew her...

He forced himself to look away from Harley and objectively observe the other people in the room.

He was standing back, watching, when he became aware that a friend had arrived.

"I have to admit I was definitely expecting you to be here," Craig Frasier told him.

Micah smiled without glancing over. "And I guess I'm not surprised that you're here," he said.

"I can't let you get into too much trouble," Craig murmured.

"I'm just here to honor an old friend," Micah said.

"Like hell." Craig smiled grimly, studying the crowd milling in the foyer. "But I don't know what you think you can discover at this late date."

Micah turned to face Craig at last, a rueful half smile on his face. "Right. Well, it would help if someone suddenly had a guilt attack and admitted going crazy—from the bacteria in the wrappings, of course—and murdering Henry."

"Not going to happen."

"I know."

"So?"

"Don't worry. I'm not going to harass your cousin," Micah said.

"I'm not worried. I think you two can actually do each other some good it you get a chance to really talk. Maybe you can figure something out, late as it might be. There was so much done so quickly and so politically. State Department, international bull. A cover-up. Yeah, it'll be good for the two of you to talk."

"You say that as if you doubt the official line, too," Micah said quietly.

"Because I do. I believe it was a cover-up."

"Not by the government," Micah said.

"By?"

Micah looked at him and said, "By Alchemy."

Craig didn't get a chance to respond.

Arlo Hampton took the microphone on a small portable dais set in the center of the foyer. He cleared his throat, then said, "Ladies and gentlemen, friends of the museum, friends of science and exploration, and friends of the City of New York!"

It took a moment for everyone to stop talking and start listening. Someone tapped a champagne flute with a fork or spoon. Then the room fell silent.

"We welcome you to our amazing new exhibit, brought to us through the genius of the man—the brilliant, kind, ever-giving man—whose name will now grace our museum walls, Dr. Henry Tomlinson. Those who knew Henry loved him. He was a scholar, but he was also a very human man who loved his family and friends. No one knew Egyptology the way Henry did…"

A sudden gasp from the crowd silenced him. Everyone turned.

Someone had come up from the basement steps, and was now staggering through the crowd.

Someone grotesquely dressed up in a mummy's linen bindings, staggering out as if acting in a very bad mummy movie.

A performance for the evening?

No.

Because Arlo grunted an angry "Excuse me!" and exited the dais, walking toward the "mummy" now careening toward him.

"What the hell?" Micah and Craig were close enough to hear Arlo's words. "Richter, is that you? You idiot! Is that you?"

It wasn't Richter; Micah knew that right away. Richter was far too big a man to be the slight, lean person now dressed up.

Or at least Ned Richter was!

Micah burst forward, phone out and in his hand. As he neared the mummy, he was already dialing 9-1-1.

"Get those bindings off her! Get them off her fast!" he commanded.

The mummy collapsed.

Micah barely managed to catch the wrapped body sagging to the floor.

As quickly as he could, he began to remove the wrappings.

He heard the sound of a siren.

Then Vivian Richter looked up at him, shuddered and closed her eyes.

The wrappings, Micah knew, had been doused in some kind of poison.

Chapter Two

Chaos reigned.

Harley was stunned and horrified that Vivian Richter was so badly hurt—so close to death.

She was wrapped tightly. The outer wrappings were decayed and falling apart; they'd come from a historic mummy. The inner wrappings were contemporary linen, the kind the museum used in its demonstrations, made to look like the real deal.

Vivian was gasping and crying, completely incoherent. One woman in the room was a doctor—a podiatrist, but hey, she'd been to medical school. She was kneeling by Vivian, calling the shots, talking on the phone to the med techs who were on their way.

Special Agent Fox had already taken control of the room. No one was to leave; they were all in a lockdown.

She was incredibly glad that Craig was there.

And, of course, he was with his girlfriend or
fiancée—Harley wasn't sure what Craig and
Kieran called each other, but she *was* sure they
were together for life. Kieran was standing near
Harley, ready to comfort her, as the slightly
older and very protective almost cousin-in-
law. Harley appreciated that, even though she
didn't really need it. She worked with criminals
all the time, as well as people who weren't so
bad but still wound up in the criminal justice
system. She was calm and stoic; Micah and
Craig were questioning people, grouping them,
speaking to them, both digging for answers and
assuring them all that they were safe.

"She's going to die! She's going to die!"
Simone Bixby, Henry Tomlinson's niece, cried
out. Harley saw that Micah Fox hurried over
to her, placed a comforting arm around her
shoulders and led her to a chair.

By then, of course, museum security had
arrived. So had the police—New York City
and state police.

People were talking everywhere. Micah and
Craig had herded everyone into groups, de-
pending on their relationship to the museum.
Some were employees of the museum; some
were special guests. The people who'd been
on the expedition were in a corner. Harley was
with Belinda Gray, Joe Rosello, Roger East-

man and Jensen Morrow, as well as the Alchemy Egyptologist, Arlo Hampton.

Ned Richter was crouched on the floor, at his wife's side.

All of this seemed to go on for a long time, yet it was a matter of minutes before more sirens screamed in the night and the EMTs were rushing in. Ned Richter was allowed to go with his wife; Arlo Hampton and others more closely associated with the exhibit were now gathered together in a new group. Guests who'd only recently made it through the doors were questioned and cleared.

Anyone who had anything to do with prep for the evening was in another group; every single person would be questioned before being permitted to leave for the night.

Officers and crime scene techs were crowding through the museum, heading to the Amenmose section—and to the staff office and prep chambers beyond.

"Too bad we couldn't continue the celebration," Joe said, hands locked behind his back, a look of disappointment on his face. "What a waste of great food and wine."

"Joe! What's the matter with you?" Belinda chastised.

"Come on! Vivian Richter's a drama queen," Joe said.

"She might die," Roger said very softly.

"You mark my words. She will not die," Joe insisted.

"They're saying it's poison," Roger pointed out. "Some kind of poison on the wrappings."

"She's going to be very, very sick," Jensen said. "Those wrappings decaying and falling all around her... Who the hell knows where they came from—or what might be on them?"

"Or if something was *put* on them," Roger said. "That's how she would have been poisoned."

They were all silent for a minute.

"And then dead—like Henry Tomlinson," Belinda said.

Again, they were silent.

"Great. But at least now, maybe someone besides me will start fighting to figure out what happened to Henry," Harley said quietly.

She'd actually discovered that night that someone *was* on her side. The agent with the great voice. Craig's friend. Micah Fox.

"Okay, okay," Belinda said. "I didn't push it a lot at the time. I mean, it didn't make any difference, did it? The cause of death—two medical examiners said—was the fact that bacteria made him crazy and he killed himself."

The reaction to her comment was yet another bout of silence.

"What were we going to do?" Belinda wailed. "We had no power. Insurgents were bearing down on the camp, and everyone wanted us out! So, what *could* we do? Henry was dead," Belinda said.

"And back then, none of us believed he killed himself," Jensen said at last.

"But we all let it go." Roger sounded sorrowful as he spoke. "Except Harley, and we all kind of shut her down," he added apologetically. "But, seriously, what were we going to do? There were some whacked-out insurrectionists coming our way. I'm sorry, but I've got to admit I didn't want to die. I really didn't care if anyone was collecting evidence properly—all I wanted was out of there! And in the end, I guess we bought into the official—" he made air quotes with his fingers "—version. It was just easier and—"

"Ms. Frasier!"

Harley was being summoned. She saw that it was the plainclothes detective who had apparently been assigned to the case. He was lean and hard-looking; his partner was broader and had almost a baby face and a great smile. They were McGrady and Rydell, Rydell being the guy with the smile.

She wasn't going anywhere alone. She was never sure how Craig could home in on her problems so quickly, and tonight he was with Micah Fox, the agent who had called her before—and approached her at the beginning of the evening. What if she *had* talked to him when he'd wanted to?

Could tonight's disaster have been avoided?

Did it have anything to do with what had happened before?

She was led into one of the museum offices that had been taken over by the police. She felt, rather than saw, her cousin Craig and the enigmatic Micah Fox come in.

They didn't sit; they took up stances behind her.

McGrady took the seat behind the desk and asked her sternly, "Ms. Frasier, what exactly is your association with the museum, the expedition—and the injured woman?"

"I was on the expedition. I don't really have an association with Vivian. It's not like we have coffee or hang around together and do girls' night," Harley said. "Vivian is married to Ned Richter, the CEO of Alchemy. Alchemy financed the expedition. Alchemy is the largest sponsor for this exhibition. We were all pretty close in the Sahara—not that we had much choice."

"So you did know her well!"

"I didn't say I knew her well. We were… colleagues."

"But you like mummies, right? All things ancient Egyptian?" McGrady asked.

"Yes, of course. I find the culture fascinating."

"And it would be a great prank to attack someone and lace her up in poisoned linen. Like a mummy?"

"What?" Harley exploded.

McGrady leaned forward, wagging a pencil at her. "You were the one who discovered Henry Tomlinson—dead. Correct?"

Harley had never thought of herself as particularly strong, but his words, coming out like an accusation, were too much.

She heard a guttural exclamation from behind her. Craig or Micah Fox, she wasn't sure which.

But it didn't matter. She could—and would—fend for herself. She leaned forward, too.

"Yes. I found Henry. A beloved friend and mentor. I found him, and I raised an outcry you wouldn't believe. And no one in a position of power or authority gave a damn. First, it was oh, the insurgents were coming! Saving our lives was more important—and yes, of course, that was true—than learning the truth about the death of a good man. I could buy that! It's an obvious decision. But then, no decent autopsy, and his niece, bereft, had him cremated. And now you're asking me about Henry—and about Vivian Richter. You have nerve. I was here tonight in honor of Henry. I didn't see the exhibit before tonight. I haven't been associated with Alchemy since we returned. I suggest you speak with the people who *were* involved there and worked on the exhibit."

McGrady actually sat back.

Everyone in the room was silent.

Then Harley thought she heard a softly spoken "Bravo."

McGrady cleared his throat. "Sorry, Ms. Frasier, but you do realize that Vivian Richter is dangerously close to... Well, we might have a murder on our hands."

"You *do* have a murder on your hands. Dr. Henry Tomlinson was murdered. Now we have to pray that Vivian comes out of this, but still, you've got a killer here. Do you have anything more to ask me?" Harley demanded. They did need to hope and pray for Vivian, but by now, surely they had to recognize the truth of what had happened to Henry!

"Did you see Vivian this evening?"

"No."

"But you arrived early, didn't you?"

"Only by a few minutes. I walked out to the temple area."

"Which is off-limits until after the exhibit officially opens tomorrow."

"I was allowed to go back there because I'd been on the expedition."

"And you were close to the backstage area where exhibits are prepared?"

"Yes."

"Where Vivian would have been?"

"Possibly."

"But you didn't see her. Who did you see?"

"Just Jensen. Jensen Morrow. He's working here, with the exhibit. This is actually his field of work. I saw Jensen—oh, and Special Agent Fox." She glanced back at him. He and Craig were flanked behind her like a pair of ancient Egyptian god-sentinels. They almost made her smile. Not quite. She couldn't believe that this detective was quizzing her—when she couldn't get any help before, no matter how she'd begged and pleaded!

"Special Agent Fox?" McGrady said.

"I arrived within minutes of Ms. Frasier. I was told she'd just headed for the temple. I wanted to speak to her about the death of Henry Tomlinson. I went straight there. We were speaking when her colleague Jensen

Morrow appeared. Exactly as she indicated," Micah Fox said.

McGrady stood up. "Fine. Ms. Frasier, you're free to go."

Harley stood up and glared at him. "I'm delighted to leave. But perhaps first you'd be kind enough to let me know how Vivian's doing. We might not be close, but we were serious associates."

McGrady sighed. "She's holding her own. The doctors are combatting the effects of the poisoning."

"What was the poison?"

"It's an ongoing investigation. That's information we can't give out right now, even if we had it."

"I see. Thank you."

Craig opened the door; she marched out. He and Micah followed. She thought she heard McGrady mutter, "And take your Feds with you."

"Not the usual helpful attitude, at least not in my association with the NYPD," Craig said. "Usually, we have an excellent working rapport."

"Maybe he's resentful because he's not sure what this is yet. It's impossible at this time to say what happened," Micah said.

Harley spun around to stare at him. "What

are you, a fool?" she snapped. "We both know—not suspect, but *know*—that Henry Tomlinson was murdered. Then Vivian Richter comes out wrapped in mummy linens, screaming and poisoned with some kind of skin toxin, and we don't know what happened? Obviously, someone tried to kill her!"

Craig grabbed her by the shoulders. "Harley! Stop. Micah's on your side. What are you?" he asked. "A fool?"

She flushed uneasily. They were just outside the door. The nicer cop, the quiet one with the baby face, Rydell, came out and approached Jensen Morrow. He was next on the block, Harley thought. And how stupid of the cops. Jensen had been with her, away from the camp, when Henry Tomlinson was killed. They just didn't seem bright enough to realize that there was a far bigger picture here. They needed to see it—before someone else died.

But Craig was right. She shouldn't be taking it out on Micah Fox.

Why was she being so hostile, so defensive? Pushing him away on purpose.

He was trying to help her. He was…

He was a promise she was afraid to accept. He claimed he wanted the truth, and he seemed to have all the assets needed to get at that truth. He was too damned good to be true, and she didn't dare depend on someone like that when the very concept of an ally, someone to depend on, was still so...

Foreign to her! He was law enforcement—and on her side. It was good. After all this time, it felt rather amazing.

"Sorry," she murmured.

She'd barely spoken when Kieran Finnegan came hurrying up next to her. "I have a car outside. Come on, I'll get you home."

"But—"

"There's nothing else you can do here tonight, Harley," Micah said.

"Remember, you came to me."

"Yes. And there's nothing else you can do here tonight," he repeated.

Harley stiffened.

"Let's go," Kieran said gently.

So she nodded. "Thank you," she said to Craig and Micah, and then she allowed Kieran to lead her out the door, to the front of the museum.

A light-colored sedan was waiting, just as Kieran had promised. Kieran wasn't driving; Harley assumed the driver was FBI and that Micah or Craig had made the arrangements.

Once in the car beside Kieran, Harley regretted the fact that she'd already left. "I should still be there. I should be back with the exhibits. I should see the prep rooms. I was with them on that expedition and I know what we discovered. I saw the tomb when it was opened. And I... Lord, yes, I'm the one who found Henry."

"Logically, there isn't a damned thing you could've done tonight. They won't let anyone back by the exhibits, the prep rooms, the offices—anywhere!—until the crime scene people have gone through it all. Naturally, everyone's hoping that Vivian Richter pulls through. If she does, maybe she'll be able to remember something that will help. For now, well..."

"McGrady is NYPD. He isn't letting Craig and that Agent Fox in on anything."

"They'll get in on it. Trust me. Craig will talk to his director. His director will call the chief of police or the mayor or someone, but they'll get in on it," Kieran said with assurance.

Harley leaned back for a moment, suddenly very tired. She closed her eyes and then opened them again, looking over at Kieran. She liked her cousin's girlfriend. Really liked her. She wasn't sure why they weren't engaged or married yet, but...

Kieran, of course, knew all about what had gone on during and after the expedition out to the Sahara in the search for Amenmose's tomb. Considering what she did for a living—a psychologist who worked with law enforcement—nothing much surprised her or rattled her. Besides, she'd met Craig during a period when the city was under siege with a spate of diamond heists.

"So tell me—what's your take on this?" Harley asked Kieran. "Who would kill Henry Tomlinson? Or rather, who'd dress up as a mummy to kill him, and then dress Vivian Richter like a mummy to try and kill her?"

"The incidents might not be related," Kieran said.

"Oh, please! Don't tell me Henry wasn't murdered! Don't tell me I want that to be the case because I don't want to believe he went crazy and committed suicide."

"I'm not saying that at all. Here's the thing. You were in the desert, so it had to be someone there. Henry's dead and maybe this would-be killer is playing on that. Or maybe the two are related. The problem is, I don't know anyone involved. It's hard enough to make judgment calls when you've had a chance to speak with people and question them."

"Yeah, yeah, I'm sorry."

"That said…"

"Yes?"

Kieran smiled and shrugged. "You've had as much education as me, if not more."

"Ah, but in different courses! I need more in psychology."

"Specifically in human emotions. Like jealousy."

"Jealousy? As in…someone who wanted to be a famed Egyptologist?"

"Possibly. Some people kill because they're deranged. They're psychotic, or they're sociopaths. Then, of course, you have the usual motives. Love, greed, hatred…jealousy. Think about everyone involved if you're convinced that the two situations are related. The rest of us weren't there. Only you know the dynamics among all the people who were on that expedition."

"I can't imagine anyone who would've wanted Henry dead. I just can't."

"It's not that you can't. It's that you don't want to," Kieran told her.

They'd reached Rector Street and the old warehouse apartment that legally belonged to Harley's uncle, who was mostly out of state now and had generously given the large, rent-controlled space to Harley while she finished her degree and decided on her permanent vocation.

The driver hopped out of the car, opening

the door for Harley. Kieran leaned out to say goodbye and thank the man.

"Get on home, get into bed, go to sleep," Kieran said. "Much better to start fresh in the morning."

Harley gave her a quick hug and a peck on the cheek. "Thanks. Thanks for getting me here. But… I'll be back on it in the morning."

Kieran grinned. "We'd expect no less." She leaned back in the car and the driver shut the door. He offered Harley a grave nod, and waited until she was safely at the door to her building.

Harley keyed open the lock and waved to the night clerk on duty at the refurbished twenty-floor building. Then she took the ancient elevator to the tenth floor. It wheezed and moaned, and she wondered if Mr. Otis himself had seen it installed in the building. However, it worked smoothly, and she was soon on her floor and in the spacious area she knew she was incredibly lucky to have in New York City. The building had once housed textile machinery and storage. She had over a thousand square feet with massive wall-length windows that looked out on the city with a special view of Grace Church. Harley knew she was blessed to have this space, and reminded herself to send Uncle Theo another thank-you. A counter separated the kitchen from the dining area and living room, while wrought iron winding stairs led up to the open loft space that was her bedroom. Her mom had told her that the apartment had once been Uncle Theo's bachelor pad, but at the ripe old age of sixty-five, he'd met Helen, the love of his life, and they were happily enjoying the pleasures of Naples, Florida, year round. Helen, a spring chicken of fifty-five, was delighted that Harley was watching over the place, just so they'd have a place to crash when they came up to see friends.

Harley found herself staring out at her view of Grace Church.

Home, bed, sleep.

Impossible.

Henry Tomlinson, an Egyptologist by trade, had loved Grace Church. The church itself dated back over two hundred years, although the current building went back to the 1840s, with new sections added along with the decades. Gothic and beautiful, it was the kind of living history that Henry loved.

She wondered if Vivian Richter was still hanging on. She thought about calling the hospital, but they probably wouldn't give her any information.

Home, bed, sleep.

She could try.

Climbing up the stairs to her bedroom, she quickly changed into a cotton nightshirt and crawled beneath the covers. She realized she hadn't closed the drapes.

She stared out at the facade of Grace Church.

Yes, Henry would have loved a view like this.

What was Henry's niece, Simone, thinking tonight?

And Micah Fox? How had he arranged time off? How had he managed to be there? Would he figure something out?

She prayed for sleep, but her mind kept returning to that time in the Sahara. Being part of the expedition had been such a privilege. She remembered the way they'd all felt when they'd broken through to the tomb. Satima Mahmoud—the pretty Egyptian interpreter who had so enchanted Joe Rosello—had been the first to scream when the workers found the entry.

Of course, Henry Tomlinson was called then. He'd been there to break the seal. They'd all laughed and joked about the curses that came with such finds, about the stupid movies that had been made.

Yes, people had died during other expeditions—as if they *had* been cursed. The Tut story was one example—and yet, by all accounts, there had been scientific explanations for everything that'd happened.

Almost everything, anyway.

And their find...

There hadn't been any curses. Not written curses, at any rate.

But Henry had died. And Henry had broken the seal...

No mummy curse had gotten to them; someone had killed Henry. And that someone had gotten away with it because neither the American Department of State nor the Egyptian government had wanted the expedition caught in the crosshairs of an insurgency. Reasonably enough!

But now...

For some reason, the uneasy dreams that came with her restless sleep weren't filled with mummies, tombs, sarcophagi or canopic jars. No funerary objects whatsoever, no golden scepters, no jewelry, no treasures.

Instead, she saw the sand. The endless sand of the Sahara. And the sand was teeming, rising up from the ground, swirling in the air.

Someone was coming...

She braced, because there were rumors swirling, along with the sand. Their group could fall under attack—there was unrest in the area. Good Lord, they were in the Middle East!

But she found herself walking through the sand, toward whomever or whatever was coming.

She saw someone.

The killer?

She kept walking toward him. There was more upheaval behind the man, sand billowing dark and heavy like a twister of deadly granules.

Then she saw him.

And it was Micah Fox.

She woke with a start.

And she wondered if he was going to be her salvation...

Or a greater danger to her heart, a danger she hadn't yet seen.

Chapter Three

Micah did his best to remain calm and completely in control. That was definitely a hard-won skill from the academy.

It was the crack of dawn, the morning after the event, and he'd been called in to see Director Richard Egan. Alone.

Egan was Craig's immediate boss. The man was Hard-ass, Craig had told him, but in a good way. He had the ability to choose the right agent for the right case in the criminal division.

He'd also fight tooth and nail when he thought the agency should be involved. He'd take a giant step back, too, when he thought he'd be interfering with the local authorities.

They were often part of a task force, but it didn't seem there was going to be one in this situation. Hell, there might not even be any official FBI involvement. At the moment, they were looking at what might have been a murder thousands of miles away, and what might have been an attempted murder at a museum opening. It might also have been some kind of bizarre ritual or prank.

Several morning newspapers—among the few still available in print—were on Egan's desk. The front pages all held stories with headlines similar to the first one he read: Mummies Walk in New York City!

Egan glanced at the papers and shook his head, dismayed, Micah thought, more by people's readiness to believe such nonsense than he was by the disturbing headlines.

"You see? Everyone will be going crazy. Thank God that woman didn't die—thank God she didn't die, no matter what—but with this mummy craze…there'll be pressure. The press will not give it up. So. Let me get this straight," Egan said. "You have lots of leave time?"

"Yes, sir. I'm on leave now."

"But you started off taking some of that leave and traveling to Egypt."

"Yes, sir." He hesitated. "That was a year ago. I took several weeks then, and I'm taking several more now. I'm never sick. I've accrued other time as well and work with a great group. So, last year…"

Egan was waiting.

"I came back. I'd heard that Henry Tomlinson, an old friend, had died under unusual circumstances. I tried to reach the site, but when I got there, it had been cleared out. I tried to track down his body, but I was behind by several steps. But you know all this." He hesitated. "I'm a bit of a workaholic, sir. Like I said. I put in a lot of time, and wind up owed a fair amount of time off."

"And you use your leave working, I see."

"I flew all over last year, being given the runaround. Our people in Cairo helped, but they were stonewalled, too. And a lot of the time, certain Egyptian officials acted as if I was an idiot and an annoyance. According to them, they were trying to keep people alive and I was making waves about a dead man. It was too late for them to do anything, of course. I pursued it as far as I could, but Henry's niece had been told that her beloved uncle had died in a horrible accident and, abiding by his wishes, had him cremated. Can't autopsy a pile of ashes."

"Our people in the Middle East would've done exactly what you did," Egan assured him.

"Yes, sir."

"But?"

"But I knew Henry Tomlinson," he said. "He was a friend. He was also a good man. His death deserved a decent investigation, which—due to the circumstances, I know—he did not get."

Egan was quiet for a minute.

Then he said, "And you just happened to be at the museum tonight when a woman, wrapped in would-be old linen tainted with nicotine poison, came crashing into the ceremony."

"So that was it, nicotine poisoning. Hmm. But I didn't just *happen* to be at the event, sir. I was there purposely. As I said, I knew Henry Tomlinson. I loved the guy. I was there to honor him."

"But Craig Frasier has an involvement because his cousin Harley was on the expedition."

Micah shrugged, but kept his eyes steady on Egan's.

"You're a good agent, Micah," Egan said after a moment. "I've seen your service record. I know your supervisor."

Micah lifted his hands. "Sir—"

"Yeah, whatever, forget about it," Egan said flatly.

"Begging your pardon, sir, but—"

"I heard the cop on the case is a dick." He grinned. "In more ways than one."

Startled, Micah raised his brows.

Egan laughed. "The guy's partner, Rydell, actually called me. He wanted to apologize for McGrady's behavior. I guess the guy was hoping it would turn into a murder case and that it would be his—and he wanted the FBI out of it."

"I see."

"Don't worry. The FBI is in. Taking lead."

"Really?" He'd decided to stay calm, so made a point of not betraying his surprise and delight.

Egan leaned back, studying him. "The case began in the Middle East. It entails far more than the City of New York."

Micah felt his pulse soar, but he still maintained his composure.

"That's excellent, sir. And…"

"Yes, I've spoken with your office. You and Craig can take lead on the case. Mike— you know, Craig's partner, Mike?—he needs some vacation time, and if you're here and we're taking this on, I'm going to go ahead and give it to him. So it'll be the two of you. Work with the cops, though, and any other agencies that may become entangled in this. We'll have State Department and embassies involved, too, I imagine. Anyway, our victim from last night regained consciousness thirty minutes ago. I've asked that they let you and Craig do the talking. You are no longer on leave. I suggest you get moving."

"Yes, sir, absolutely. Thank you."

"Just get the son of a bitch," Egan said.

Micah nodded and started out.

"Hey!" Egan called, stopping him.

"Sir?" Micah walked back.

"I didn't hear much about that whole mess in Egypt. What ever happened with the insurrection?"

"Over before it began, from what I understand," Micah told him. "By the time I landed in Cairo, the expedition people were on planes headed out. And the military had routed the coup—it was more of a student protest than anything else. Sadly, it's a fact that there's a lot of unrest in the Middle East, for various reasons. Anyway, it was over, but the expedition was gone. I went out to the site, but...by then, there was nothing to find. Everything had been cleaned out."

"And the insurgents?"

"A few arrests. Most of them dispersed when the military came on the scene."

"In retrospect it might look like overkill, but better safe than sorry," Egan said.

"Of course, always," Micah agreed.

But as he left Egan's office, he found himself wondering, for the first time, whether the insurgent event had been planned to ensure that Henry Tomlinson's death wasn't investigated.

Maybe he was pushing it, getting paranoid.

Maybe he was taking a conspiracy theory too far.

And yet…

Had there been some kind of conspiracy?

"WHAT DO YOU THINK?" Jensen asked Harley.

She was back at the museum, in the Amenmose exhibit; she hadn't been able to resist. Jensen had called her, saying that with Vivian in the hospital, he could use some extra help, so she'd come.

"They've delayed the opening by a day," he'd told her over the phone early that morning. "But with Vivian out of the picture—temporarily, of course!—and especially since you were there and have a memory like a camera, you can help me with loose ends, tying things up, paperwork."

She'd assured him that she'd be there.

Jensen had told her he'd never left the museum the night before. He didn't look tired, but he was one of those people who could work for days, then sleep twenty-four hours, party a night away, and work a full load again. Jensen could be absolutely tireless.

"I think the exhibit is so special. Just like Henry," she said quietly.

They were standing in the temple area, right where she'd stood the night before when Micah Fox had come upon her. But she wasn't staring at the exhibit, which was surrounded by the glass-and-concrete walk and the "river"; rather, she was looking back at the hall that led to the temple.

One broad corridor led here, with six smaller chambers off the main hall. The temple faced east, in the direction of the sunrise, since it was dedicated to the sun god, Ra. It wasn't filled with statues. Instead, it was open to the glass that revealed the sun.

"The earliest known temple to Ra," Harley said, smiling.

Jensen nodded. "Info on Ra, on Tutankhamen, Ay and Amenmose are on the side there. Near Amenmose's mummy." That was on display in a small room, which it had all to itself. "The hallways feature a lot of the fabulous funerary art we found," Jensen continued.

"Which is surprising, don't you think?" Harley asked.

"How do you mean? That we have anything

left—after running out with our tails between our legs?"

"Running out with our tails between our legs was the only thing to do," Harley replied. "No, of course, the historical assumption is that Amenmose was murdered. By someone under Ay, who knew that Amenmose wanted to usurp his power with the boy king, Tutankhamen. Our discovery proved that he *was* murdered, once we were back in the States and the body was properly identified through the DNA testing."

"He'd been strangled!" Jensen said.

"Like Henry," Harley murmured.

"Well, we don't really know about Henry."

"I do."

Jensen shrugged. "In this case," he said, "when it comes to Amenmose, X-rays that show fractured hyoid bones don't lie."

"But we have no clue who did it."

"I'm willing to bet Ay did it himself."

"Oh, today, in one of our courts, Ay would be guilty. He'd be guilty of *conspiracy* to commit murder. It was his idea, I'm sure. But that's just it. Somehow, Amenmose still ended up being properly mummified and placed in an inner coffin and several sarcophagi and laid to rest in his tomb. So who killed him? And who got the body and managed to bury it with such honor?"

"Hey, I'm the Egyptologist here!" Jensen reminded her.

"Yes, and I'm the criminologist. We've got to know who did it and why," Harley said lightly.

"I think we can rest assured that the murderer has long since gone to his own reward," Jensen said, grinning.

"Amenmose's murderer."

"Ah! But not whoever murdered Henry, right? Is that what you mean?"

She nodded.

"Your cousin's FBI and that other guy, Micah, he is, too. They'll get to the truth. And now, because of what happened to Vivian, they'll keep going," he said with confidence. "And guess what? We sold out. We didn't open today as planned, obviously, but we will tomorrow…and it's a total sellout. Not that sales weren't good before, but now that we have mummies walking around, we're a real hit."

"I've seen the news and read a few of the papers. Yeah, what a great story. But there was no mummy walking around. That was Vivian. And speaking of her, how's she doing? Have you heard anything?" Harley asked.

"Doing well, I understand. Awake and

aware and lording it over the hospital staff. She's going to be fine."

"Thank God. But what's she said?"

"Nothing. She remembers nothing. Who knows what'll happen eventually? They'll have shrinks in there and everything. At the moment, though…nothing."

"But she'll be okay. That's the most important thing."

"Of course," Jensen agreed. Then he said, "So, what are you doing tonight?"

"What am I doing?" Harley repeated. She felt a strange tension. She'd almost dated Jensen when they were on the expedition. Almost. There was nothing to dislike. He was good-looking, he was smart, he was alpha-fun and…

She did like him.

But she suddenly dreaded the fact that he might be asking her out. There wouldn't have been anything wrong with dating Jensen. They'd teased and they'd flirted and come close. But now she wanted to retreat; she wasn't sure why. It must be everything that had happened, that *was* happening…

She didn't want to turn him down. She wanted to be friends. Maybe she even wanted the relationship option left open.

"I'm, um… I'm not sure," she said. "I

came here this morning because you said you needed me, and I want to help."

"This is social."

"Oh. Well, um—"

He laughed softly. "Don't worry. I'm not putting you on the spot. Not tonight. We wanted the whole group to get together. Those of us who were the last people with Henry," he added.

"Oh. Okay. Well, you know that my cousin's girlfriend owns a place and—"

"Yes! That's right. What a great idea! Finnegan's on Broadway. We were planning on meeting somewhere midtown, but once you're on the subway, who cares? We talked, Belinda and Joe and Roger and I. And we thought we owed it to ourselves and to Henry to have our own private little event. Can you get us a corner at Finnegan's? A reserved corner?"

"Anyone can make reservations. But—"

"But you'll be someone they care about when you make the reservation."

"It's a pub. That means hospitality. They care about everyone."

"But more about you."

She gave up. "No problem. I'll make the reservation."

"Cool. So you'll join us all?" Jensen asked her.

"Sure. It'll be great."

Would it be great? she wondered. What was going on with Vivian now? The woman hadn't died; she was doing well. If that had changed, surely they'd all know.

And the majority of the museum was open, although there was a little time left for the cops to come back and look over the new stuff for the Henry Tomlinson section. Still...

"Love ya!" Jensen said, grabbing her by the shoulders and planting a quick kiss on her lips. "I'm so glad you're in for tonight! I was afraid that you wouldn't be."

"Nope, I'm in," Harley assured him. "Anyway, I thought there was work you needed me to do?"

"Yeah, look around the exhibit. Some of the work here is yours, like the prep stuff you were writing up before we even found the tomb. For someone who was going into criminology, you were quite the Egyptologist."

"Hey, lots of people do more than one thing in life. I love Egyptology. It was my minor, just not my major."

"That's my point here. Thing is, check it all out. Make sure there are no imbecilic mistakes."

"Okay. But I'm not the most qualified person to be doing this."

"Oh, come on! You *should've* been an Egyptologist. You were so good at all the stuff we delved into. You knew who thought what, all about the argument over the gods, everything. And you cared about what we were doing. You just wanted to do more with fingerprints and DNA and the detecting part of it. But this exhibition is your baby, too. Check it out for me. You're going to love it!"

He waved and started walking in the direction of the temple, then apparently decided he should go the other way. The temple was a dead end, except, of course, for museum employees. There was a back hall that led to the stairway and a number of museum offices.

"Where are you going?" she asked.

"To clean up—after the cops!" he told her.

"Clean up what?"

He didn't hear her or pretended not to. But he wasn't heading to his office. She had no idea what he was up to.

She glanced at her watch.

That was all he wanted? For her to verify exhibits? He'd said he'd needed help because Vivian wasn't there. And yet he didn't really need much.

Did it matter? She'd never get a chance like this again.

She wasn't even part of it all anymore; she

was Jensen's guest and she was a guest because once, she *had* been a part of it all. She didn't embrace Egyptology with the same wonder that drove some of the others, but she did love ancient Egyptian history.

Nope, she probably wouldn't have another opportunity to wander the exhibit entirely alone.

For a moment, she stood still, and then she smiled. She hurried to the right, slipping into one of the rooms where the social and political climate of Amenmose's life and times were explained. She'd done a great deal of the research work and prepared a number of the papers from which the story in the exhibit had been taken.

Entering the first room, she looked around. Display cases held many items of day-to-day life; sure, there were fantastic necklaces and beautiful jewelry, but Harley had always been most fascinated by the storage jars, the pans and other cooking implements that told more about a basic everyday lifestyle.

The center in this exhibit was an exceptionally fine statue of the god Ra, depicted with the head of a falcon, the sun disc above him.

She read softly aloud. "'Ra—ancient Egyptian sun god. By the fifth dynasty, in the 25th to 24th centuries BC, he had risen to prominence, and would be joined by others at various times. Tutankhamen's great changes after his father's reign and his own ascension to the throne involved bringing back the old religion. Under Akhenaten's rule, the old gods had been disrespected; many statues and other honorary sites were destroyed. His dedication to his religion—he wanted to see the deity Aten, the disc of Ra, the sun god, worshipped above all else—caused a weakness in the Egyptian military and a lack of action that was seen as a betrayal by a number of the kingdom's allies. Tutankhamen meant to undo the harm, as he saw it, his father had done. He wanted to bring back all the old gods, including Amun and Mut and others who made up the hierarchy of ancient Egyptian power. Amun-Ra, as Ra was often called, and the others would return. Tutankhamen felt his father's legacy was one of destruction, and under *his* rule, the world would improve. To that end, he looked to the priest Amenmose, despite the fact that the priest Ay was in power as the boy king's regent.'"

She let her words settle in the empty room. "Pretty good," she said with satisfaction.

There was an inner sarcophagus of a handmaiden, buried with Amenmose, in the last of the horseshoe-shaped displays. The woman, at least judging by the artist who had painted her face for the sarcophagus, had been beautiful.

"What do you think?" she asked the image of the long-dead woman. "The New Kingdom, Middle Kingdom, Old Kingdom—it can all be so confusing. Not to mention the dynasties! Anyway, I think the display works, and I had a lot to do with that. It's simple enough to be understood, without leaving out any important facts. Of course, in my view, young King Tut was probably murdered, too. But we'll never find out now, since Howard Carter found that tomb so long ago!"

She read the little note beneath the sarcophagus. The young woman's name had been Ser. She'd served Amenmose in his household. She hadn't been killed for the purpose of being placed in his tomb. She'd succumbed to a fever before his death, and had been moved here to lie with the man she had served so loyally.

Next to her was a servant, Namhi. Like Amenmose, Namhi had been strangled. There was no explanation anywhere on his wrappings or in the tomb. From all that she had read, Harley suspected that either Namhi had been used as an instrument of murder, or he had belonged to the cult of Aten-Aten, a secret society pretending to agree with Tutankhamen's return to the old religion while trying to undermine it at the same time. It had been suspected during Amenmose's lifetime that Namhi was a leader of the cult. That alone would make Ay want to murder him, as well as Amenmose. But Amenmose might also have been murdered by Tutankhamen's half sister or brother-in-law.

Ay had actually been the grand vizier. And, upon Tutankhamen's death, he would become pharaoh.

"You all had motive," Harley murmured.

Yes, just as it seemed everyone did today in the murder of Henry Tomlinson and the attempted murder of Vivian Richter. No one had a solid motive—or, rather, they all had the same motives! Fame, position in life, in society. But…was that enough to make someone kill?

Harley turned to look at the case where mummified animals were displayed. She was staring at a mummified cat when she heard the bone-chilling sound of a cat screeching as if all four paws and its tail had been caught in a car door.

She froze; she felt goose bumps forming all over her body.

There were no cats in the museum. Not living cats, anyway!

A complete silence followed the sound. And then Harley became certain that she heard movement in one of the side rooms off the Amenmose exhibit main hall.

She remained still, listening.

She'd spent her life priding herself on her logic. Obviously, a mummified cat had not let out a yowl. It was more than possible that someone else was in the exhibit. And possible that a cat had somehow found its way in. There might well be police in the prep areas and in the offices behind the public areas of the museum.

Despite her logical reasoning, there was no way to explain the sensations she was feeling. They were different from anything she'd ever known.

She quickly slipped from the side room where she'd been, the first one next to the temple. She thought she saw movement at the end of the hall.

A person, wearing something dark.

That hall was a dead end for visitors. There was a magnificent podium that held the giant-size lion sculptures that had guarded the inner door to the Amenmose tomb. You walked around it and saw the second side of the exhibit before exiting to the rest of the museum.

She told herself she had no reason to be

afraid that someone was there. People worked here, for heaven's sake! The cops and crime scene techs were probably still trying to figure out how Vivian Richter had been assaulted with nicotine poison.

But...

There'd been something furtive about the dark figure.

Well, at least it hadn't been a mummy walking around. The person had definitely not been in decaying and frayed linen wrappings.

Whoever it was wore black. Head-to-toe black. Slinking around.

Crazy!

The room she was in displayed different stages of mummification. There was a life-size display in which a mannequin was being dried with natron on a prep table, while priests said their prayers and sprinkled him with some kind of herb water or oil. In the next window, the wrapping process itself was displayed.

The next room was filled with sarcophagi and mummies, wrapped, half-wrapped and unwrapped. And among them...

She paused again, gazing at Unknown Mummy #1. She suddenly, vividly, remembered the night Henry had died. She could see the interior of the prep tent, could see Henry, his face reflecting his enthusiasm.

Somebody brushed by something out in the hallway.

Anyone might have been there! Working, investigating, exploring.

No. The person was moving…

Furtively.

She hurried to the door and looked outside. She could run back to the statues and escape into the back to the offices and prep rooms behind the scenes.

She could demand that whoever it was show him or herself.

And wind up with a belt or other object around her neck, or poisoned linen wrapped around her body?

She realized that her heart was thundering. In a thousand years, she could never have imagined being so frightened in the middle of the day in a museum. She wasn't sure she'd been this frightened even when they were forced to flee the Sahara.

Harley flattened herself against the wall, waiting.

She was startled to hear the scream of a cat again.

That was no damned mummy! There was a living cat in the museum—fact!

But she wasn't staying to search for it.

She burst out into the hallway, racing toward the exit.

"Harley!"

She heard her name; it was a heated whisper. She sensed somehow that it wasn't a threat, but by then she was propelling herself forward at a frantic pace.

"Harley!"

That whisper of her name again.

She wasn't going to make the exit.

She turned and saw Micah Fox standing there.

One minute she was running, her feet barely touching the floor.

The next...

She'd fallen flat on her back, blinking up at the man straddling her.

"Harley! Damn!"

Fox. Micah Fox. Special Agent Micah Fox.

She stared at him blankly. For a moment, she wondered if *he'd* been stalking her through the Amenmose exhibit.

"There was someone in here!" she said. "Watching me."

"Yes," he said flatly. "And thanks to you, that someone has gotten away."

Micah rose to his feet and helped Harley to hers. "What?" she demanded. "How?"

"I had him—or her. I don't even know which it was. Then you made enough noise to raise a legion of the dead—"

"Oh, no, no, no! *You* were the one making the noise!" Harley told him.

"Harley, if you'd just stayed where you were…"

"And let someone get me? What a bright comment from a law enforcement officer!"

"Harley," he began, then broke off and halfway smiled, lowered his head and shook it slightly. "Sorry. I guess I think of you as Craig's cousin, and as a student of criminology, and I suppose…"

"You suppose what?"

"That you'll behave as if you were trained in criminal behavior and…well, working a case."

She stood there, still staring at him, pursing her lips. Then she offered him an icy smile. "Okay, let's put it this way. Take doctors. Some are great practitioners and others are diagnosticians. My training helps us to figure out what happened—not to bulldoze our way into a situation with guns blazing!"

He listened to her speak; his reaction was undeniable amusement.

"Okay, whatever. Let's go to the offices here and see who we can see, yes?" he asked her.

She turned and headed for the doors marked Cast Members Only—as if they were at a theme park rather than a museum—and pushed her way in. She feared for a moment that the doors would be locked. They were not.

A long hall stretched before her. To the left were offices; to the right were the labs and prep rooms.

She could see that one door was marked with the name Gordon Vincent. She hadn't really met him, she realized, and he wasn't just in charge of the Amenmose exhibit, but the entire museum. His appearance was perfect for the part; he was solid, about six feet even, gray-haired and entirely dignified. The office beside his bore a temporary name; that was obvious from the way the name placard had been slipped over another, the name being Arlo Hampton. Next to his office, the jerry-rigged nameplate read Vivian Richter.

Jensen Morrow had his own office, since he was now an employee of the museum.

No one was in the hall. Looking through the large plate-glass windows to the lab, they could see that Arlo wasn't in his office; he was in the lab. He was working with one of the unnamed mummies they'd found in the tomb, running the X-ray machine over the remains. Harley waited until he'd completed his task.

Then she tapped on a window. Arlo raised his head, startled. He saw Harley and offered her a large smile—then noticed Micah and didn't seem quite so pleased. He disappeared for a moment as he walked through the changing area and then opened the hallway door to let them in.

He beamed; in fact, he seemed to come alive as he met Harley's gaze.

He did not seem concerned that a woman, a colleague, was in the hospital. That someone had attempted to murder her in a particularly grotesque manner.

"Harley, nice to see you. Jensen said he asked you to come in. I believe he was going to ask you to work with him on a few last additions we're thinking of adding. I'll tell you the truth, I wish you'd been one of ours. I want a room on what we've discovered from the mummies—and what we know about their deaths. Oh, the whole Tut thing is still speculation, and that's not ours to tear apart. This is!"

"Thanks," Harley said, wondering why Jensen hadn't mentioned that. "I'm happy to help with…whatever's needed."

"Great. And you, Agent Fox." Arlo turned to him. "Are you part of the police investigation? They were here all night. They found nothing. Of course, they still have Vivian's office closed off and we won't open this section until tomorrow, but...wow."

"Yeah, wow," Micah said, his tone flat. "So, what do *you* think happened to Vivian Richter?"

"Her husband's with her now," Arlo said. "I mean, needless to say, we care most about the living. It's just that...well, the world can't stop because something bad happened to someone."

"Yeah, but that bad thing happened right here," Micah reminded him.

"Of course," Arlo said. "But...it had to be a prank, right? She didn't die. I'm thinking some college student who suffered some kind of slight at our hands was in here and played a prank on her."

"Nicotine poisoning is no prank."

Arlo looked truly perplexed. "Someone definitely came in through the back, to get to her. Otherwise, whoever it was would've been on the cameras. The only people picked up on the security video cameras in this section were the two of you and Jensen Morrow. But, of course, there are entrances from the basement on up—a few secret entrances. Did you know the building itself was originally erected by Astor as a bank? That's why there's the gorgeous foyer and all. But speaking of secret entrances, the cops are looking at everything. Oh yeah, you're a cop. Okay, sort of a cop. Do you want a tour?"

"I would love a tour," Micah told him. "But first, who else is working today?"

"Well, define 'working.' I think everyone's been in. The only one not really part of the new exhibit is Harley. Belinda, Joe and Roger have been giving it about ten hours a week. Jensen is here full-time, which I'm sure you know. Joe and Belinda both have full-time jobs with two of the other major museums in the city, and Roger is teaching now. They were all in at one time or another this morning, checking out their space. The cops tore through everything, looking for the source of the wrapping and the poison. But honestly, I don't think we even have any natural linen back here. And any idiot knows that's not how you make an ancient Egyptian mummy. But—"

"So who else was here this morning, Arlo?"

"Let's see. Ned Richter was in. Left the hospital, popped over here and went back. But he was here."

"And the others?" Harley asked.

"Yes, like I said, at one time or another. I've been busy, as you can see. We still have a wealth of remains and artifacts. There was the mess with that so-called insurgent group, but then the company and the government sent guys with big trucks and equipment, and they emptied the tomb—including all the mummies—before thieves could. Oh yeah, some people see the Western world as one giant thief, but everything we have is cleared through the Egyptian government and will be returned, and that was common knowledge from the get-go."

Arlo seemed to consider it more important to honor international agreements than to worry about anything else.

Admirable.

But Henry had died. And Vivian might have died, too.

"I'd love that tour now," Micah said, smiling. Harley saw the way his face moved when he smiled. Obviously, despite his work, he smiled a lot. He had the kind of smile that made her wonder what it would be like if they were just talking together at a restaurant, in a class...

"I can't give you a tour of the entire place. We're going to concentrate on this exhibit. You'll notice that our offices are in this section with the directors, with Gordon Vincent. He's a very smart, well-educated and supportive guy. He purposely keeps his office over here. That way, whatever is new, he's in on it."

"So he might have been in his office before Vivian came out screaming?" Micah asked.

"I suppose so," Arlo replied. "But are you suggesting Gordon was involved? Really? I don't think so."

Harley didn't, either. He hadn't been on the expedition. She could tell that Micah didn't think Vincent was guilty of anything, either; he was just covering his bases.

"Show me around, please. That would be great," Micah said.

"Okay, let's go!"

Arlo ripped off his paper lab coat and set out. "As you can see, that's a lab—a 'clean room' lab, if you will. You have to coat up, glove up and mask up before going in. You never know what might've been in the ground for millennia! And over there, the museum offices. Now, we're on the ground floor, or so you'd think. Directly beneath us is the cafeteria and there's another rotunda-like area for international exhibits. That one's a bit different. International, of course, but Egyptology has always had a place in the higher echelon of what people find fascinating in a museum. And, sadly, museums are bottom-line—everyone needs donations and funding and numbers—and mummies are a draw. Always have been. Even though they were so plentiful in Victorian times that people used them for kindling! Yes, those good religious uptight folk used human remains as kindling."

He kept talking, pointing out different research rooms and more offices. Then he came to a staircase. It was an old stone circular staircase, high and steep. "This led down to the vaults at one time. It wouldn't have been easy to steal from this place when it was a bank!"

They followed him down to the basement and then the sub-basement.

"Does this bypass the actual basement?"

"Yes, these stairs do. And…" Arlo turned, shining a flashlight at them, although they were still receiving ample light from above. "It'll get dark in here!" he warned.

Harley took a penlight from her purse at the same time as Micah drew one from his pocket. She was rather proud of herself for never leaving home without one!

"You can still kind of see. There was emergency lighting put down here before the place went belly-up during the Great Depression," Arlo told them. "As you can tell, the design of the hallways is almost like a perfect cross, and each of them opens out to five vaults. The elite of the elite had their treasure down there.

The museum will use the space eventually, but at this stage, it's not really needed yet. Anyway, the quality of the exhibits means more than the quantity."

Arlo was quite happy to keep talking. They saw what he meant about the cross design, and each section held vaults of slightly different sizes.

"And there's a way out?" Harley asked.

Arlo didn't get a chance to answer. There was a narrow area that simply looked like an empty space at the end of the vault area facing Central Park. Micah headed that way.

Harley followed Micah, and Arlo followed her.

"What's going on?" Arlo asked when Micah came to a stop.

Micah had found something. Harley could hear metal grating and squealing; she realized he'd come to a door. That he'd gotten it open.

She came up behind him and looked over his shoulder.

All she saw was black.

"Abandoned subway tunnel. They're all over the city," he murmured.

"I guess that's one way out. Or you can just walk out the door that leads back up to the park and picnic area at the side of the museum," Arlo said, pointing to the right. "But an abandoned subway. I think I'd heard rumors, but never really knew if they were true of not. Cool!"

"Yeah. Cool," Micah said wryly. "So, does everyone know about that way out—to the park area?" he asked Arlo.

"Oh, I wouldn't think so," Arlo replied. "Just people who work here. And maybe people they've told."

"We might want to get a lock on the door to that exit," Micah said. "And to the subway tunnels. The info could easily have been tweeted across the country. Maybe it has." He paused, studying Harley. "We'll get a few of our people down here," he told her. "I need to go over to the hospital. I've been told that Vivian is conscious and speaking. But I'll need to find you later. Do you know where you'll be?"

Harley hesitated. Then she shrugged. "Finnegan's," she told him. "Finnegan's on Broadway."

"Kieran's family's place?" he asked her.

"It's the only Finnegan's on Broadway."

"You'll definitely be there?"

"Oh, yes. I'll be meeting my colleagues from the expedition."

"Including me!" Arlo said happily. He sighed. "Well, we won't have Vivian there, and I doubt we'll have Ned Richter with Viv in the hospital."

"Henry. We won't have Henry," Harley said.

"No, we won't have Henry," Arlo agreed. He tried an awkward smile. "But at least we won't have any mummies running around at Finnegan's. A banshee or two, maybe, but no mummies!"

Neither of them managed even a small smile for his attempt at humor.

As they left, Harley remembered the cat she'd heard earlier. There'd been no further sound after Micah had appeared—claiming she'd frightened off the person who'd apparently been stalking her. The person he, in turn, had followed. And lost.

Chapter Four

"I was in my office," Vivian Richter said. "I was in my office…"

Her voice trailed off. Her face was set in a concentrated frown.

"In my office and then…"

"And then?" Micah pushed gently.

Vivian was in her hospital bed, in a seated position. Craig Frasier and Micah stood at the foot of the bed, patiently waiting.

Micah knew that the local cops had already been in. But it had only been a short time since the lead on the investigation had been handed over to the federal government. Vivian had let them know that she'd spoken with McGrady and Rydell. The nurse in the hallway had informed them that McGrady had brought Vivian to tears, demanding that she remember what she just couldn't.

Micah had received a call from Rydell,

since it was still a joint task force, if a small one. Rydell had apologized for his partner.

For the most part, I work with great people. No one is better than the NYPD, Rydell had assured him.

Micah had told him not to worry; any agency in the world could come with a jerk or two—and McGrady was that jerk. He hadn't said that in so many words when he'd spoken to Rydell, but they both knew exactly who he was talking about.

"I'll bet you were excited about the exhibit," Micah told Vivian. "All the work that had been done. And then the discovery—and the terror in the desert, with Henry Tomlinson dead and the fear of armed rebels coming at the camp. But now, here, you have the culmination of your dream of getting the Amenmose exhibit up!"

"Oh, I was excited. So excited. And we were going to have all our grad students and Henry's niece and her family at the opening. And…oh! Those children. Henry's great-nieces and nephews. And there were probably other children there. And they saw me coming out like—?"

"A mummy. Vivian, think. Did anyone come in to see you in your office when you were getting ready for the grand celebration?"

Her frown deepened.

"Everyone had been there. Everyone. Ned, of course. We were excited together. He's administration and I'm an Egyptologist, but we're a married couple, and that made it an incredible night for both of us. Arlo, darting in and out with last-minute things. The grad students…they were all there. Belinda wanted me to look at her dress and Joe—that boy is such a flirt!—asked if he looked both dignified and handsome. Let's see, Jensen. He's full-time here now, you know. He was in more than once. And then…"

She went silent, dead silent, her mouth falling open in an awkward O of horror.

"What?" Craig asked.

"One of the mummies came in. It was walking. Yes, yes, that was it! There was a mummy. Oh, my God! A mummy… I remember now. It…stared at me!"

She began to shake. Micah and Craig glanced at each other, deciding it might be time to hit the nurse-call button.

But first they both moved close to her, each man taking one of her hands.

"It's going to be all right," Micah said in a soothing voice.

She shook her head. "Mummies don't walk. Except in really bad movies. Okay, even good movies… *The Mummy* with Brendan Fraser was good." She paused. The shaking had stopped, and she looked at Craig. "You any relation?"

"I'm afraid not. My last name's actually Frasier," Craig told her.

Vivian suddenly stared hard at Micah. "That was it, yes. I saw the mummy. I stood up—I'd been at my desk. I stood up, and I couldn't believe what I was seeing. It had to be a joke, a prank…but then the thing came at me and I tried to scream, or I think I did, and it kept coming…and…"

"And?" Micah asked.

"That's it. That's all I remember. A mummy came to life," she whispered.

"Vivian, you of all people know that a mummy didn't come to life. Whoever was pretending to be a mummy wrapped you in linens that had been soaked with nicotine. That person wasn't a real mummy," Micah said.

"But…it seemed so real. Or surreal. But terrifying!" Vivian said.

"Vivian, someone who was in the museum at the time dressed up as a mummy to attack you. Do you have any idea why? Were you having an argument with anyone? Is there any reason— Well, I'll be blunt," Craig said. "Is there any reason anyone would want you dead?"

Vivian gasped. "Oh, God!"

Micah glanced at Craig. She must have just realized that someone had tried to kill her.

"No, no, no!" Vivian said. "I know I'm not the nicest human being in the world. I'm not a Pollyanna of any kind, but… I don't hurt people. I've never fired anyone, not that I have that kind of power. I'm not mean to people, I don't scream at them to work harder. I'm a decent person, damn it! No, there's no reason anyone would want to kill me!" she declared.

"Did you have a fight with anyone—anyone at all?" Micah asked.

She sighed. "Every once in a while, I get into it with Arlo. But that's just because…well, when Henry was alive, we all acknowledged him as the real guru. He had the experience. He was chosen by Alchemy to head up the exhibition, and he was chosen because all his research on Amenmose was so good and so thorough. With Henry gone, I think maybe Arlo and I have a bit of a rivalry going. But a healthy rivalry!"

"Arlo was working today."

"Of course he was. There's still much to be done. You have to understand that the tomb was *filled* with mummies, including that of

Amenmose. And, as with Tut, some of the funerary objects appear to have been reused. We have every reason to believe that Amenmose was murdered—and it must've happened quite suddenly. He was entombed with all the rites by someone who really loved him, but it was all hush-hush and under the radar. Ay did become the ruler after Tut died. Anyway, there's still so much to determine about our find! I'm sure everyone's working." She was quiet for a minute. "Including my husband. Bless Ned. He was so torn! But I've assured him that I'm on the way to being just fine and that the museum—at this moment—is the most important thing in our lives right now. And I'm getting great care here, so it's fine that he's gone."

Micah wasn't sure she was telling the truth. He wasn't convinced she didn't feel hurt that her husband wasn't with her.

But he didn't want to rub salt into any wounds.

He glanced at Craig. They would move on. Craig was probably doubting her words, too, but they wouldn't get different answers to what they'd asked—not at the moment. Time to ask other questions.

"What about the grad students? Any arguments with any of them?"

"Well, they're not grad students anymore, are they?" Vivian asked a little sharply. "I told you, I saw Belinda and Joe and..." She paused, sighing deeply. "I was a bit worried about seeing your cousin, Agent Frasier. She was so committed to Henry. We all loved him, but it was as if he saw her as a grandchild and she saw him as a wonderfully brilliant grandpa. She never got over his death. Then, of course, there's Jensen, and he's taken a permanent position with the museum. He helped her fight for Henry up to the end, and then... Henry was cremated. We had two different medical examiners give verdicts that suggested suicide, possibly brought on by a delirium caused by bacteria. Anyway, we'll probably never know just what was going on in Henry's mind. And..." She broke off again, looking from Micah to Craig. "Someone wanted me dead, too. But how did I get out in the foyer? How did I get help? Oh, it's all so terrifying!"

She began sobbing quietly.

Micah squeezed her hand. "Hey, you're going to be fine. So if there's anything, anything at all, please call one of us. We intend to find the truth. We *will* find the truth."

She nodded and squeezed his hand back. "Thank you," she said.

"Of course," he told her.

He thought she smiled.

THERE WAS A lively crowd at Finnegan's on Broadway that night, but then again, it was Friday.

New Yorkers had a tendency to be "neighborhood" people. On the Upper East Side, you found an Upper East Side hangout. There were lots of bars and pubs around Cooper Union, St. Mark's Place, the Villages, East and West, and any other neighborhood you could think of in the giant metropolis.

But Finnegan's drew people from everywhere. For one thing, it was one of the longest-running pubs in the city, dating back to pre–Civil War days. For another, it was run with a family feel, and somehow, people knew the right time to bring their kids and the right time not to. The kitchen was as important as the bar. It was simply a unique place, and Harley was delighted with Craig's association with the Finnegan family—and through him, her own connection to them.

She'd been able to reserve a corner near the entrance, against the wall and across from the actual bar tables.

Jensen got there first, greeting her with a hug and a kiss on each cheek. She wasn't sure

just how far he would have gone; a waitress—
a lovely girl who'd just arrived from Ireland,
came by to take their order. That was when
Joe Rosello walked in.

He had to flirt. But he couldn't seem to de-
cide whether to flirt with Harley or the waitress.

He opted for both, which got him a punch
on the shoulder from Jensen. "Hell, you can't
take him anywhere."

"You are atrocious," Harley told him, shaking her head.

"Hey! I just admire people and make them
happy. I don't do anything evil!" Joe protested.

"We'll let it slide this time," Jensen said.
"Lay off Harley, eh? She's seen you with the
ladies. She knows your MO."

"Harley, do you really mind me telling you
that you're gorgeous and mysterious and desir-
able in black?" Joe asked, sounding wounded.

"No, just don't slobber on my hand, please."

"Slobber? That was an elegant kiss!"

"Ah-ha! A very wet and elegant kiss!" Jensen said. By now, Roger had come in; he listened to the ongoing conversation, rolling his
eyes. "And every one of us has a doctorate!"
he murmured. "Pathetic. What is this world
coming to?"

"I think the world was a mess long before we came along!" Belinda said, joining them.

It was then that Harley noticed Micah Fox; she hadn't seen him come in. He was standing at the bar with her cousin Craig. The oldest Finnegan, Declan, who ran the family establishment, was talking to the two men.

She had a feeling they were all watching her and her friends.

A minute later, Micah walked over and joined the group.

Harley wasn't the first to greet him; Belinda was. Harley was busy greeting Arlo, who had just arrived, and Ned Richter, who had apparently chosen to join them rather than stay with his wife at the hospital.

They were seated around two of the big mahogany tables in the corner, Ned Richter, Arlo, Joe, Roger and Belinda crowded in against the wall, and Craig, Micah, Harley and Jensen perched on the chairs across from them. There was ordering of drinks and meals, with casual conversation at first. And then Ned Richter raised his glass and said, "In memory of Henry Tomlinson, the greatest Egyptologist I ever knew and one of the finest men to have ever walked this earth, as well."

"Hear, hear!" the others chimed in.

They all raised a glass to Henry, and then

Ned continued with, "And to the bastard who hurt my Vivian—may these agents and cops find him, and may he rot in hell!"

"Hear, hear!" another cry went up.

"That's harsh," Jensen teased. "At least you're among friends."

"That's what an Irish pub is all about," Richter reminded them all, drawing a round of laughter. He went on, saying, "Sorry, I can't help it. I hope the bastard dies a hideous death."

Harley wondered why he wasn't with his wife, since he was so devastated by what had been done to her.

But she was wedged between Jensen and Micah, and she was very aware of both men being so close to her. She found herself wondering, too, just what connected people. She was seated between two very fine men. Both exceptionally good-looking and bright—and both engaged with the world...in completely different ways.

She liked them both.

And yet, sitting there, she knew why she wasn't with Jensen, why they hadn't gone out. Each man's interest was unmistakable.

But only one man's seemed to matter.

She was attracted to Micah Fox. She barely knew him, and yet when she'd seen him again, just the sound of his voice had aroused her senses.

"Seriously, who would've done such a thing? Harley, what do you remember?"

Harley realized that her mind had completely—and inappropriately—wandered. Belinda was staring at her, brown eyes wide, and waiting for an answer.

Harley took a sip of her drink—a Kaliber nonalcoholic beer by Guinness, since she'd decided she couldn't risk losing an ounce of control tonight. She hoped someone would say something that explained Belinda's question.

She felt Micah's eyes on her. Maybe he knew she'd been distracted. Hopefully, he didn't know that her mental absence at the table had been due to him.

"About that night…that night in the Sahara," he said.

"We were all so excited," she began, and around her, Jensen, Joe, Roger and Belinda all nodded.

"And we were rewarded!" Ned Richter said.

"A find beyond measure!" Arlo agreed.

"We'd started to bring some things from the tomb into the prep tent," Harley said. "It's a special tent, temperature-controlled. Everyone's careful there. Amenmose's tomb turned out to have more than a dozen mummies and sarcophagi—all in different states of disrepair and decay. We've proven that Amenmose was murdered, so after it happened, someone who loved him borrowed—or stole—funerary objects from the dead who'd passed on before him. They also brought together people, dead and alive, who'd served him."

"Why would they do that? Why go out and find people who'd already died to bury with him?" Micah asked her. "I studied Egyptology," he said sheepishly, "but, I don't understand—taking people who have already died and their things. It's like robbing the dead. It *is* robbing the dead."

"He would need servants in his next life. Servants, women… He would need people and animals, just as he'd need his bow and shield," Harley explained.

"I know about objects needed for the next life. I guess I never heard of them being taken from somewhere else…dead, or still alive."

Micah seemed to move even closer to her. She could feel his eyes; she could almost feel his touch. His elbow was on the table and his fingers dangled near her lap.

She forced herself to concentrate. "We worked really hard that day—for hours and hours. I'm pretty sure it was close to eight o'clock. There was a little village not far from the dig and the people there were incredibly nice. We'd go sometimes to have dinner and maybe sit with coffee at a place there, something like a family-run restaurant or cantina. But we decided in the end that Jensen and I would go by ourselves and bring back food. Jensen came to get me while I was trying to talk Henry into coming with us. We were all tired, of course." She glanced over at Belinda who was still watching her with wide brown eyes. "Belinda was Skyping with Al. he was in Iraq at the time, I think."

"Iraq, yes, just about to leave," Belinda said.

"And Roger was working on tech and communications because we were hearing rumors about an upstart hate group, so he didn't go." She turned to Joe and couldn't help grinning. "Joe was still moving some of the artifacts. We had a lovely young Egyptian as our interpreter. Satima Mahmoud. They were…working."

"Working, right!" Belinda mocked, then laughed affectionately. "Joe was flirting."

"What? I don't flirt!" Joe protested.

"You're a flirt!"

Harley was sure they all said the words at the same time.

Joe flushed and shrugged. "She's really pretty. And smart."

"That she is," Harley agreed.

"So, Jensen," Micah said, looking past Harley, "you and Harley went out together that night. How long were you gone?"

Jensen thought it over, raising a brow at Harley. "Hour and a half maybe?"

"Somewhere in there. An hour to an hour and a half," Harley said.

Micah nodded, then swiveled around to look at Ned Richter and Arlo Hampton. "Neither of you checked on Henry during that time?"

"There was no need to check on Henry!" Ned Richter said. "We had security on the outskirts of the camp. Henry was completely in his element, like a kid in a candy store. I wouldn't have interrupted him."

"And you?" Micah asked Arlo. "Shouldn't you have been in there with him?"

"No, because I—"

Arlo turned beet red and stopped speaking.

"You what?"

"I was working," Arlo said.

"On what?" Ned Richter demanded.

Arlo looked guiltily around. "Well, I had one of the funerary tablets in my tent."

"You took a tablet from the find into your tent?" Ned repeated, his tone grating.

"Well, you see, I was interpreting, trying to

figure out just what had happened at this site and how. It wasn't usual, having that many dead in a tomb. I was transcribing the tablet."

"What did it say?" Harley asked. She'd never heard about the tablet.

Arlo flushed miserably again. "I don't know."

"No artifacts in private tents," Ned told him, irritated. "I'm not going to fire your ass or anything over it, but damn it, that's the last time, Arlo. We follow the rules at Alchemy."

"What did the tablet say?" Harley persisted.

"I don't know," Arlo said again, his expression peevish.

"You didn't translate?" Harley asked.

"I didn't have time. I got through a zillion lines of how wonderful Amenmose had been and then...you started screaming."

"I'd just found a friend—dead!"

"Well, yes, you screamed, and then everyone had to come and look at Henry. Then we heard we were about to be attacked, and *then* we were all helping when it came to loading up what we could, trying to get to the airport in Cairo."

"Yes, but where—"

"Harley, I haven't the faintest idea where the damned tablet ended up!" Arlo said. "I thought we were getting together tonight to be supportive, and you're all accusing me of terrible things!"

"We didn't *accuse* you," Ned pointed out drily. "You admitted you took an artifact."

Arlo sighed. "Where were *you*? What were you doing? Why wasn't Vivian with Henry? She's the one who loves it all so, so much!"

"I had gone to get dinner to bring with Jensen. And, then, of course, when we got back, we were busy making plans to get everyone and everything out of the desert! That was a nightmare. What the hell? We're going to attack one another now?"

"Hey, guys, you all came here to honor Henry!" Micah reminded them.

Jensen laughed. "You're the one who started this."

"Yes, I am," Micah said seriously. "Henry died out there that night. Now Vivian's been attacked. I wonder if you realize just how lethal nicotine poisoning can be."

"I certainly realize," Ned Richter said hoarsely.

"We all do. It's just that...we wouldn't have hurt Henry!" Belinda said. "And... I have no idea what went on with Vivian. No idea," she repeated softly.

"Nor do I. She was in her office," Jensen said.

"And you last saw her when?"

"I told the police—I told anyone who asked. I saw her about an hour before the celebration started. She was in her office, said hi, then waved me out. She seemed too busy to worry about the opening ceremonies, although she definitely showed up later. She loves the exhibit, you know."

"The rest of you? Did anyone see her before the celebration?" Micah asked.

"I saw her at about four o'clock," Ned Richter said. "She came to my office. She wanted permission for more expensive testing. I told her we had to hold off for a while." He paused and then added, "Every once in a while, I have to make her understand my position. I'm a CEO. I can't give in to her just because she's my wife. *Especially* because she's my wife. She's a highly qualified Egyptologist, but she didn't even work for Alchemy at first. She has her position due to me, so..."

"I waved to her," Arlo offered. "I was working in the lab. She didn't wave back. She was concentrating on whatever she was doing. Then again, that's Vivian's way."

"I didn't see her at all," Belinda said. "You know, not until..."

"Me, neither," Joe said.

"Nor me," Roger chimed in.

"Thanks." Micah lifted his glass. "So, to

the evening, then, huh? To Henry, our mentor, a man we all loved dearly... I assume?"

Assent was quickly voiced by everyone in the group.

"To Henry!"

Their waitress came by; Harley noted that Micah made a point of dropping any questioning at that point. Instead, he ordered the pub's very popular shepherd's pie.

He clearly had the ability to be very charming when he chose. He got Belinda to speak about her upcoming marriage—she was supposed to have a Christmas wedding—and he got Arlo talking about the way he'd fallen in love with mummies at the Chicago Field Museum as a kid. Joe, in his turn, became enthusiastic and wistful talking about the beautiful Satima Mahmoud and what an excellent interpreter she'd been, helping whenever anyone needed it. They'd come this close to having an affair, he admitted, and then, of course, everything had gone to hell.

Roger talked about his love for the desert—and his happiness over the fact that they were home. There was no place like New York. He loved being home, he said; he loved his job.

Ned didn't stay more than an hour, since he was going back to the hospital to be with his wife.

No one else seemed to want to break up their get-together, but it was growing late. The fine Irish band playing that night announced their last number.

The evening inevitably came to an end.

"So who sees to it that our lovely companions get home okay?" Joe asked, rising and indicating Belinda and Harley.

"No need to worry about me," Harley assured them. "Seriously. The tall, dark, handsome and deadly-looking guy at the bar is my cousin."

"Oh, Craig's here! I didn't realize. He should've joined us," Belinda said.

"Maybe he didn't want this to look like an inquisition," Jensen said, staring at Micah.

"Maybe," Micah said casually. The two men were almost the same height, both about six-three. Micah was smiling, not about to get into it—and not about to back down.

"If you're tired, I can take you to your place," Jensen told Harley.

"I'm fine, really," she said. "My cousin, remember? Craig is my cousin."

"Yeah, he is," Jensen said. For a moment, his eyes fell on her, and she thought he might be feeling something like jealousy over her preference for Craig's company rather than his. But although they'd teased and flirted, they'd never dated; they'd never been more than friends. She liked that he was protective. However, he didn't have any grounds to be jealous. At least not of Craig…

"Fine. Belinda?" Jensen said.

She laughed. "I'm a native New Yorker. I've been taking the latest subway most of my life. But sure."

"Your fiancé is a man serving his nation, Belinda. It's my privilege to see you safely home. And," he added, "I'm damned good with the subways myself."

"Okay, thanks. Come on. I'll make tea when we get to my place—so you can get yourself safely home after that!" Belinda left with Jensen's arm around her.

Harley realized that, as the others trailed out, she was still standing near the exit with Micah.

"Strange," he muttered.

"What is?"

"He's the one person who can't be guilty."

"Who? You mean Jensen?"

Micah turned to look at her, studying her eyes thoughtfully, his own pensive. "Yes. He was with you in the desert. The two of you saw Henry alive together, and then you left together, and when you came back, Henry was dead."

"Yes. Why do you find Jensen suspicious?"

"Something about him."

"They teach you that at the academy?" Harley asked.

"Actually, yes. But never mind." He took her elbow. She was startled by the way she reacted to his simple touch.

"Shall we join Craig?" he asked.

They did. Craig stood politely to offer Harley his bar stool, but almost on cue, the cuddling couple who'd been taking up the seats next to him rose, hand in hand, seeing nothing but each other. They began to wander from the bar and toward the exit. Craig gestured at the three stools conveniently left for them and they all sat down.

Micah went over the conversations at the bar and Harley knew that Jensen had been right; Micah really had been grilling all of them.

If Craig had joined them, it wouldn't have been a get-together.

It would've been an inquisition, just as he'd said.

Kieran came from the back office, sliding in comfortably with her back to Craig's chest, leaning against him on his bar stool.

"Make any headway?" she asked.

"Ah, yes, Special Agent Fox has had a gut feeling," Harley replied.

"I don't trust the guy," Micah said mildly. "Jensen."

"Hmm," Kieran murmured.

"The psychologist's deep, dark 'hmm'!" Craig said. "There must be a Freudian meaning there!"

"No, I don't think there's a rational explanation for a gut feeling." Kieran shook her head. "But perhaps if there's dislike involved..."

"Don't dislike the guy. He seems okay. But I sense that he's not quite trustworthy," Micah said.

"Ah." Harley shrugged. "I have a hard time seeing Jensen as a criminal. And in our group, Joe's the one who tends to go off on tangents, not that it means he's guilty of anything. But he's easily distracted."

"By the beautiful Egyptian girl," Micah said. "Satima Mahmoud."

"Yes, and she's still in Egypt, so I doubt she had anything to do with last night," Harley said.

"You know for sure that she's still in Egypt?" Micah asked.

"I, um..."

Harley was forced to pause. "No. Of course

I don't know *for sure* that she's in Egypt. I assume she is. It's where she lives and works."

"Worth checking on," Micah said. He was, however, aiming the remark at Craig, who nodded in agreement.

"I think I need to go home." Harley stood up, yawning.

"I've got a car today. We'll get you home," Craig said. "Kieran? You ready?"

"You guys go ahead. I promised Declan some help figuring out an invoice."

"No, it's okay! I go home alone all the time," Harley said. "You—"

"Micah, you take the car," Craig interrupted. "Pick me up in the morning. I'll wait here with Kieran. Declan can drop us off or we'll grab an Uber."

"I can grab an Uber, too. I'm really close, just by Grace Church," Harley said.

"No," Craig insisted. "Let Micah take you, please. This whole mummy thing is…creepy."

"I'm not afraid of mummies."

"You should be. But only of the living ones," Kieran said. "Living people who are pretending to be mummies. Or having other people dress up like mummies. Anyway, get home safely, okay?"

Arguing would make her appear…argumentative, Harley thought.

"Thanks," she said simply. She turned away, aware that she was trembling slightly. It was a ride—a ride home. She wasn't afraid of Micah. She was afraid of herself.

She felt intensely attracted to the man. She'd sat at their table in the bar, wondering how she could be seated between two men with all the right stuff—and feel such an attraction to one and not the other.

She knew nothing at all about Micah Fox, except that he was with the FBI, that he'd worked with Craig and that Craig seemed to like him. And that he'd also been a student of Henry's.

That was the sum total of her knowledge. Was it enough of a basis for…anything?

Or had she spent the past year drifting, trying to develop an interest in someone, and not managing to find any kind of spark, any reason to pursue a relationship, even just a sexual one?

But if this was sexual, did it matter?

It did! He'd loved Henry, too. He was friends with Craig.

What if she threw herself at him, and he turned her down?

She was afraid her thoughts were making her blush, so she kissed her cousin and Kieran good-night and led the way, with

Micah right behind her. She explained that it was ridiculous that he felt he had to drive her; it was maybe a mile away at most.

"Yeah, but it's late," Micah said.

She knew that the cars Craig used that belonged to the bureau could be parked just about anywhere. Except that parking wasn't easy in Lower Manhattan—or pretty much anywhere in Manhattan!

"You can drop me off in front of the building, and thank you again," Harley told him.

"I don't think so." He gave her a smile. "Sorry, even if you weren't Craig's cousin, it wouldn't be my style."

"You'll never find parking."

"Yes, I will. The academy also taught us how to summon our individual parking witches," he said, his tone droll.

She pursed her lips and sighed. "Great. Witches? I thought people had parking fairies."

"Not in the academy. Witches are scarier. They get rid of the other cars, frighten them off, you know?"

He did have a parking witch—or damned good luck. She was surprised at how close he got to her building.

He walked her there, and stepped inside

with her. He saw the security guard and nodded in approval.

And, of course, he could leave her right there. She was obviously safe; her building had keyed entry and security! The push of a button summoned the police in the event of any trouble.

She found herself staring at him, waiting.

"Good building," he told her.

"Thanks."

She hesitated. She wanted to kick herself. She was standing here so casually—surely she was standing casually; surely she could speak casually!—but she didn't want to let him go. Something was alive inside her, something burning, hot, shaking, nervous…something that made her feel as if she was in her teens again. She'd done very little except study and work over the past year, trying to struggle up from the strange void Henry's death had created.

"Did you want to come up for…tea?" she finally ventured. "Or something stronger? And a view of Grace Church?" she asked. She had to sound like an idiot. "I'm keyed up tonight. I don't know why. I keep thinking we should all be exhausted…"

"Yes."

"What?"

"Sure, I'd love to come up."

"Oh! Um, great." She turned and headed for the elevators, praying that her flushed face wouldn't betray the way she suddenly longed to forget every propriety, every word, and just fall into his arms.

Preferably naked!

Chapter Five

"This place is incredible!" Micah said, looking around her loft. He glanced at her with a curious frown. "Did I miss something about you? You're a trust fund baby?"

She laughed. "I happen to have an uncle who isn't living here right now. He was a snow bird, but these days he's spending most of his time in Florida. He's had the place for fifty years, and I'm pretty sure his dad had it before him. They were both in construction, so they did a great job with the space. However, only in NYC, Tokyo, Mexico City and a few other cities around the globe would this be considered a big space. You must've tried to rent in New York at some point."

He nodded, staring out the windows at Grace Church.

"I went to Brown, and then to Columbia University, so I lived here for a while," he told her. He grinned drily. "I think I lived in a closet."

"Ah, Columbia," she murmured. "But you knew Henry at Brown, right?"

"Yep. I knew Henry. I went on to Columbia, where I was a grad student. I didn't particularly intend to be an Egyptologist, but I was considering anthropology or archeology. And then..."

His voice trailed off. He shrugged and then turned to look at her again. "My senior year as an undergrad, a friend of mine was kidnapped. The FBI tracked down the kidnappers. My friend's family was rich, and yes, they were going for a ransom. But...well, one of the guys admitted after they were caught that they hadn't intended to let him live. I guess I kind of fell into a bit of hero worship for the FBI. So, I switched to criminology. I knew I wanted to do what those agents had done."

"I'm sure you made a great choice. I know how Craig feels. Of course, my whole family worries about him, but we all believe he made a great decision."

"Yeah. Sometimes, though, the bitter truth is that you lose, too. Things don't always work out the way you want them to."

"You didn't lose with Henry. You were never in the fight," Harley said quietly.

He nodded. "Yeah? Thanks. Well, I suppose I should get going."

"I'm still wide-awake. Um…can I get you something to drink? I was going to make tea. Oh, it's not decaffeinated. I mean, that's never made much of a difference to me, but…"

"Caffeine. Sounds good."

"Okay."

She turned in her little kitchen area and put the kettle on. He perched on one of the bar stools. Facing her, he also faced the kitchen. Spinning around on any of the stools, you'd still have the great view of Grace Church. She waited for the water to boil, aware that he watched her as she got out mugs and tea bags.

She needed to let him go. And she needed to let go of her interest in him—emotional and physical!

"How's it going with Officer Friendly?" she asked.

"McGrady?" he asked. "He's kind of irrelevant. The powers that be have gotten the NYC office put in charge," he told her. "Henry's death may not be related to what happened at the opening ceremony, but on the other hand, it might have been. That makes this not just national but international, and luckily the FBI does work out of an office in Cairo. It was my first avenue of investigation last year when I heard about Henry. I wasn't officially on the case, but I went to Cairo. I knew our guys would be sympathetic. This might be a terrible thing to say, but I think Detective McGrady might've been disappointed that he wound up with a live victim. He wanted a murder case."

"You still have to deal with him, though?"

"Yes, but he's not really interested now. Rydell's a good guy, and he keeps apologizing for his partner. We haven't made any complaints. We're trying to keep it all copacetic."

"Where would someone get nicotine for a poisoning like that? I gather the linens were soaked in it and only the fact that they got them off her so fast saved Vivian's life, right?"

"Right."

The kettle whistled, and Harley poured the water into two mugs. Their fingers nearly touched as she pushed his toward him, as they both dipped their tea bags in the hot water. She flushed, catching his eyes on her.

She really, really needed to let him go.

That or…

Give in. Spit out the truth that she was incredibly attracted to him. Totally inappropriate under the circumstances, but they *were* adults, after all. It could just be sex; she could handle that. And they could try to figure out what was going on between them after this case was solved.

"We have people looking into large purchases of nicotine, but—"

"Insecticide," Harley interrupted, thinking of the most obvious place to buy commercial nicotine.

He sipped his tea and nodded. "I forgot. Research for an investigation agency is what you've been doing."

"Part-time. I've been trying to sort out what to do with my career. And this job pays well." She shrugged. "Only a few of the cases I've worked on have actually been criminal. Mostly civil suits. A lot of my time's been spent monitoring bad behavior. People trying to get a relative to leave money to one person or another, husbands and wives behaving poorly and, very sadly, in one case that did become criminal—stopping a blood relative from preying on a young boy. The job's been interesting, but I haven't been sure what I want to do, which way I want to go. But since I met Kieran, I've come to like the psychology part. I think I'd like to get into profiling."

"You certainly have the right degrees."

"It all looks good on paper. I'd have to see how I do in practice."

"Want to practice?" he asked her.

"What do you mean?"

He was suddenly very serious. "Think of all the people you know who were involved with the Amenmose expedition and exhibit. Who would have a reason to kill Henry? Was money ever an issue?"

"Not that I know of—other than the fact that an archeologist's prestige means more money the next time he or she wants to go out on a project. But I'm sure you're aware of that."

Harley realized she was leaning against the counter. He was seated in one of the stools, so that meant she was leaning closer and closer to him. Their fingers, wrapped around their mugs, were only inches away.

It was hardly champagne and strawberries.

It was...

She needed to move back.

"Ye olde process of elimination," he murmured, apparently unaware of their closeness. "So, who can you eliminate?"

"Everyone!" Harley said.

He shook his head. "That won't work. You most probably know the killer."

"Any of the students would benefit from prestige. It would make a radical difference as far as their careers in Egyptology, archeology and anthropology are concerned," Harley said. "It was impressive to work with a man like Henry, but to take his place would be even more impressive. Still..."

"Process of elimination," he repeated, then abruptly stood up.

"I have to leave."

"Oh. Okay. If you have to."

"Yeah, I do."

But he was still standing there. He smiled suddenly. "Yeah, I have to go," he said again.

"You really don't."

His smile deepened. "I do."

"Because I'm Craig's cousin?"

He shook his head, his eyes never leaving hers. "Because you're you. I don't know what it is... I guess we can't define attraction, but... Anyway, I'm being presumptuous, but—"

"No, actually, you're not," Harley broke in. She wondered how you could *feel* someone so completely when you weren't even touching that person.

"We have to give it time and thought."

"I wasn't thinking everlasting commitment. I'm not FBI, but I can help a great deal and we're going to...be together. Differently. I—"

"That's not what I meant," Micah said.

"Yes, okay. I guess I know what you mean.

I believe… I believe we'll see each other tomorrow and the next day, and if…"

"Yes," Micah said. Then, neither spoke; they looked at each other.

"We're adults," Harley whispered.

"Yes, and so… I'm heading out."

He walked to the door. Harley followed him, ready to lock up when he left. She stayed a short distance behind him. She felt as if her flesh and blood, muscle and bone, had come alive, as if neurons or atoms or other chemical entities were flashing through her system with tiny sparks of red-hot fire. He had to leave; otherwise, she'd embarrass herself.

But she didn't really care.

Still, he was right. They needed time. Just because they could hook up didn't mean they should forget that there were consequences to any deed, even if neither had any expectations.

At the door, he turned to her.

It could have all ended there—as it should have.

She could've stayed where she was.

But she didn't. She walked forward, her eyes on his, until she was touching him, and when she did, he backed into the door. At the same time, his arms came around her.

She touched his face. Stroked his cheek, felt

the power in his arms as he drew her close. She let herself shudder with a delicious abandon as she felt the heat of his body, the texture and strength in his muscles. And then she felt his mouth, crushing hers, and she returned the kiss with equal open-mouthed passion. They stood in the doorway, fumbling with each other's clothing. Micah pulled away for a second, removing his holster and Glock from the back of his waistband, setting them down on the occasional table.

Then he paused, breathing heavily. "Wait. Is there...someone else? Is there that kind of reason?"

She shook her head. "No. No one else. There hasn't been anyone else in well over a year." She felt her cheeks turn a dozen shades of red. "But it's all right. I'm on the pill."

He drew her back into his arms for a very long, very wet, hot kiss.

Then they moved through the apartment, half disrobing themselves, half helping each other.

They stood in the center of the loft, next to the plate glass windows looking out on the night, on the gothic structure of Grace Church. They both hesitated a minute.

Not that anything was wrong; rather she felt blessed.

The light that came in and bathed them together was beautiful and romantic. Micah smiled and said, "I have this great image of me sweeping you into my arms and carrying you up the stairway…but it's winding and it's iron and…"

Harley laughed. She turned and ran up the winding stairway to the loft. He quickly joined her.

The loft seemed to be aglow with light in the most glorious colors—pastels with bursts of darker blue and mauve, probably from some vehicle moving down on the street. They found each other's mouths again, kissed forever, and then Harley rolled over and straddled him. They twined their fingers together and looked at each other again, and she couldn't help wondering if it was possible to not really know someone—but to believe that you did.

You could be fooling yourself! a voice nagged.

But she didn't care. She'd been spending the year since Henry's death biding time, waiting…

For what, she hadn't known.

Until now? Until this? And maybe it was just sex…

But at this point in her life, that was fine, too!

She felt his hands moving over her body,

touching and teasing, exploring and giving. They turned on the bed, facing each other, laughing, kissing, their lips roaming, intimate. They shared kisses that caused sensation to soar, cries to escape into the night...

Then at last they were together, moving with the brilliant colors of the night. She caught his eyes and they were beautiful.

His hands were electric, his movement fierce and erotic, and it seemed that they'd joined in something wonderful that captured the pulse and beat of the city...agonizing in its wonder, lasting too long, and yet over too quickly.

She lay beside him, breathing desperately. She could hear her own heartbeat as if it shook the very foundations of the building.

And she felt his knuckles, gentle on her cheek. He pulled her to him. She prayed her heartbeat would slow...

"What are you thinking?" he asked her quietly.

For some reason, she couldn't resist being honest.

"That you're very, very good. Or that everyone else in my life of the boyfriend variety has been bad. Disappointing, anyway. I mean, as a lover..."

He laughed. "I'm going to take the 'very,

very good."' He hesitated, drawing a line gently from her face to her collarbone. "Why?" he asked.

"Why are you good at this?" she murmured, perfectly aware that wasn't what he meant.

"Why have you been...alone?" he asked her.

She shook her head. "I haven't been alone. My world is very rich with family and friends. I'm lucky. I've been out there. I've even waited tables a few times at Finnegan's when they were short on people. And I actually like working for Fillmore Investigations. I'm not out on the street much. I like to think I'm kind of a little like Sherlock Holmes. Field agents with the company bring me information and I figure things out from the bits and pieces. I often talk to Kieran, and discuss my people with her, put them in hypothetical situations."

"That's work. Not personal."

"Yes, true. I've been to Florida to visit my family. And I've gone to tons of shows with Kieran's family. Her twin brother, Kevin, is an actor and—"

"I know. So why did you suddenly need me so badly?" he asked her.

She turned toward him, drawing the sheets to her shoulders as she answered the question. "Why are *you* here—needed or just as needy?" she asked.

He laughed softly. "Ouch. Hmm."

"It's a fair question. I was in criminology, probably because of Craig. I've lost family members, but I hadn't ever seen anyone die the way Henry did. And I was so crazy about him, as if he'd been a relative. You know… yeah, you know what he was like. Anyway, I tried to do something about his death. I failed. I never expected this, though!"

"You mean me?"

"No, sorry! No, I meant Thursday night, at the gala. Vivian! Why kill Henry and wait all this time to attack Vivian?" Harley asked.

He rolled onto his back and stared at the ceiling. "Maybe the killer's triggered by events."

"You mean—"

"Henry died the day your team made the discovery. Vivian was attacked the day you were all about to celebrate that discovery."

"The mummy's curse?"

He groaned.

"No! I don't believe it, but… Micah, there were Egyptian workers who told us we were going to be cursed."

"None of the Egyptian workers were here at the gala," Micah reminded her.

"Yolanda. Yolanda Akeem," Harley said.

"Ah, Yolanda."

"You know her?"

"I do. I met her in Cairo."

"So…would you say you're friends?"

"Oh, I don't think that word describes our brief time together. No, she got me out of Egypt, helped me chase after you guys," Micah said. "We're having some problems reaching her, although I assume she's still in the country. McGrady tried to get her to stick around after the night of the celebration, and he managed to talk to her for a few minutes, but in my mind, she hadn't been properly questioned yet."

"What? Why?"

"She has some kind of diplomatic immunity. And, of course, she had nothing to do with what happened to Vivian."

"How do you know that?"

"She was always within range of cameras," Micah said. He smiled. "The FBI's taken the lead, so we have footage, prints, you name it. Sadly, even with all the crime scene evidence that was collected, we don't have answers. But as far as Yolanda goes, we're almost positive she wasn't anywhere near the museum before the gala. She arrived just in time for the party, and she was on camera the entire time. She didn't even take a trip to the ladies' room."

"Why do you think she doesn't want to talk to police?"

"Apparently, she believes that the entire expedition was run by a bunch of idiots, and she's tired of all the bad press involving archeological work in her country." He grinned suddenly, and ran a finger from her collarbone to her abdomen. "There's something wrong with this picture. I'm lying here, next to you, seeing you, feeling you and…"

"And we're talking about work. But with your kind of job, it's what you do all the time, right? Is that what you mean?"

"No," he said, laughing. "What I meant is that I'm obviously not so good or you'd be more intrigued by us being together here— naked in bed!—than by the puzzles that will return in the morning."

"Morning, evening…"

Harley felt almost giddy and worried about herself all at once. It was too natural to be here with him. Too easy, too sweet.

She crawled on top of him, her breasts just teasing his chest. "Don't worry. I'm not at all distracted. Like I said, you're very, very good. Of course, feel free to reinforce such a notion at any time."

"Of course!"

He drew her to him. They were locked in a

hot, wet kiss again, then disengaged to shower each other with featherlight touches, brushing with their lips and fingertips, delicate brushes that turned urgent and became fierce, passionate lovemaking that left them both breathless, hearts pounding once again.

It was incredible. Being together was incredible. She lay curled next to him as he held her. They were both silent for a few minutes.

"Okay, we know that while Yolanda Akeem might conceivably have had something to do with Henry's death, she couldn't have had anything to do with what happened to Vivian," Micah murmured.

Harley laughed softly. "So, *I'm* not that good, eh?"

He turned to her. "Good? Good? 'Good' is a total understatement. You are spectacular. And beyond."

They both went on to prove just how much they appreciated each other.

WHEN MORNING CAME, and they'd both showered and dressed, he sat on the bed next to her, adjusting his sleeves while she buttoned her blouse.

"Amazing, huh?" he said. "And that's not a word I use lightly."

"What is?" She grinned; she couldn't help

herself. "'Very, very, *very* good'? Now, as to amazing…"

"Hey!"

"Okay…amazing."

"I meant that it was special to have a night like this, to be focused entirely on another person, without losing focus on the rest of your life."

"But remember, neither of us has a hold on the other. How awkward! What I mean is… you didn't become forever committed."

He gently kissed her lips.

"No hold. I have to meet up with Craig at the office. I'll see you later, right?"

Harley nodded. "I'll be at Finnegan's this evening. I've gotten together with Kieran and Craig for Sunday roast the last few weeks. I imagine that if you're going to be with Craig, you'll end up there, as well."

"Excellent."

At the door, he lingered, kissing her good-bye.

He left and she leaned against the door.

Then she reminded herself that he'd been nothing but a forgotten voice until two nights ago. That she'd wanted to believe she'd be happy with just one night.

Except that now…

She wanted far more than a night.

MICAH SAT IN the New York office with Craig and one of the computer techs.

He stared at the security footage from the museum over and over again.

It didn't matter how long he studied the footage, it didn't change. He saw everyone involved with the exhibit as they arrived that day. Administrators and other key people got there early, heading straight over to the area that was about to be unveiled.

He saw the coming and going of visitors to the main part of the museum during the day.

The caterers arrived. Everything looked just as it should for the evening that would welcome a special group for the official opening of the Henry Tomlinson Collection.

"Whatever went on with Vivian, it was planned way before the event. There are security cameras just about everywhere except for the offices, and they reveal nothing and no one out of the ordinary. Of course, there are the subterranean so-called 'secret access' areas that Arlo showed Harley and me," Micah said. "There's no question in my mind that whoever did this planned it well ahead of time. The linens would've been on hand in the prep room. Even before the Amenmose exhibit, the museum offered Egyptology and they have classes for high school kids in which the religious and funerary rituals are demonstrated. As to the nicotine poisoning, it's easy enough to get hold of insecticide."

"We'll need warrants," Craig said, "if we want to check out credit card purchases. Although I sincerely doubt we'd find what we're looking for. And I'm not sure we can even get warrants unless we have information or evidence we can use to designate suspects."

"Whoever bought the poison didn't use a credit card. And he or she didn't buy it all at the same place," Micah said. "It's one of them," he added. "I know that one of them killed Henry. The same person apparently tried to kill Vivian. Either that or…"

"Or?"

"We've been chasing the wrong dog," Micah said thoughtfully. He looked at Craig. "Everyone involved in that exhibit and in the expedition knows that a lot of people didn't believe a verdict of death by accident—that Henry killed himself in a state of delirium—no matter what official reports said. I realize that most eventually gave up and accepted the verdict, or pretended to."

"What if someone was trying to kill Vivian, and trying to make it *appear* that it was Henry's killer coming after her?" Craig suggested.

"I don't know," Micah said with a long sigh.

"Maybe that's far-fetched. I'm still suspicious about the entire thing that went on in the desert. The insurgency—the supposedly violent insurgency that killed no one and led to nothing but a few demonstrators being arrested. Also, there's another name that keeps coming up, that of Satima Mahmoud. The translator."

"She's in Egypt."

"I'd like to talk to her. If we can reach someone in our Cairo office, perhaps they can arrange a meeting."

"All right. I'll give tech a call. We'll see if they can get through to our people over there now. And if so, if the staff can bring Satima in and set up a satellite call."

"That's great. Either a video meeting or, if I have to, I'll fly back over."

"Alone?" Craig asked him.

"You're welcome to join me."

"I wasn't thinking about me. To be honest, I don't like the idea of Harley going back there—not now, and not in relation to this case."

"I wouldn't bring Harley," Micah said quickly.

"You're going to make damned sure you keep her out of danger, right? I know she'd say she can look after herself, and of course, that's true. But she's my cousin and I love her, so I can't help feeling this way. You understand?"

Micah nodded. He understood.

Craig was still looking at him. "Yeah, you do understand. Thank you," he said quietly.

And once again, Micah nodded.

Chapter Six

Edward Fillmore was an exceptional boss.

In many ways—although he was less on the slightly crazy academic side—he reminded her of Henry Tomlinson.

They were both decent men. Not on-a-pedestal wonderful; they had their moments. But they were both good people. Or, rather, Henry *had* been good until his unfair and untimely end.

Edward had founded his company years earlier. They handled private investigations, such as finding lost family members, searching for missing children and were certainly happy to participate in any "silver" alert, as well. He seldom took on divorce cases in which one spouse was trying to trap the other. In fact, he'd only take on such a case if he met with someone he saw as an injured party first, and then only if it meant getting suitable support for any children who might be affected.

When Harley had first gone to work for him, he'd told her to feel free to use her own time and whatever resources the company had to look into Henry's death. She'd never used work hours—say, when she was tracking down a credit card report or some lead on a missing person—to pursue her own investigation. But she'd accepted his offer, although she hadn't come up with anything yet. Henry was gone, had been cremated. And there was no lead to follow; it was all a stone wall. It was somewhat comforting to know that the FBI had encountered the same stone wall. No one had been able to crack the defenses established when the Amenmose expedition had ended, Henry had died and they'd all left the site.

Now, of course, she had a new crime to pursue—the poisoning of Vivian Richter.

She called Edward Fillmore and asked if she might have his blessing to head into the offices and search through info on various people.

Edward was quick to allow her access to his computers and databases.

So Harley spent her Sunday morning going through everything she could find on everyone she knew—including her colleagues on the expedition, the people she'd never suspected. Her search yielded little.

Ned Richter had been a CEO with a pharmaceutical company for nine years before joining Alchemy, where he'd been in charge of "Exploration" for over a decade.

His work record was spotless. He'd graduated from Harvard.

He'd married Vivian Clifford, a graduate of Cornell, a decade ago. When not working, the couple loved to vacation in historic places, including Peru, Mexico, Egypt and Greece. The couple had no children, but seemed devoted to each other.

Arlo Hampton had no criminal record, not even a parking ticket. He'd received his doctorate in Egyptology from Brown. He'd been with Alchemy for nearly eight years and had been hired by Ned Richter.

She looked up Jensen next. He'd gone to NYU. He was a New Yorker through and through.

He had a ton of parking tickets.

Nothing else on him.

Roger Eastman had been arrested once; he'd been protesting commercial testing on animals.

He'd received probation.

Belinda had no parking tickets—she didn't drive. She'd never been arrested. She'd been valedictorian of her high school class and had gone to Northwestern before arriving in New York for graduate work.

Joe—Joseph Rosello—had also been born in New York City, in the Bronx. He'd gone to Ithaca, in Syracuse, and then finished at Brown. However, she found something she hadn't known or even suspected. He'd paid his way through college by working as an extra in movies and doing a stand-up comedy gig at a place in Times Square.

According to his social media pages, he still enjoyed dressing up and playing parts.

She should have known this. And, of course, she would have—if she'd just spent more time on social media. So…he played roles.

Would that include the part of a mummy?

HARLEY WASN'T EVEN sure what she was doing at first when she reached for the phone; then she knew. She called Kieran and asked for Kevin's number, since Kevin was a working New York actor.

Naturally, Kieran wanted to know what was up. Harley told her.

"Kevin's performing at some kind of zombie walk today in Times Square. What's your guy's name? I can see if he's taking part," Kieran said.

But Harley didn't need Kieran to check it out for her; she'd keyed in some more information and had come up with Joe's status for the day.

"Yes!" she exclaimed. "They're both taking part in the zombie walk. The walk's for charity, and Joe's one of the performers doing pictures with people. Hey, do you feel like heading down to be in a zombie walk?"

"Sure," Kieran said. "I'll be a good sister. What the heck, we can support a charity and investigate what's going on. Sounds like a plan to me."

They agreed to meet at a restaurant off Times Square—quieter and not as much of a tourist attraction—and get lunch before joining the zombie walk.

And watching the players.

A waste of time? Harley wondered.

A lot of investigative work was a waste of time; that was part of the process of elimination, as Micah had described it. But Kieran was right. If nothing else, their entry fees would go toward charity.

MICAH HAD NO intention of denying anything; he really cared about Harley—and Harley certainly behaved as if she cared about him. Was it forever and ever? How could they tell? Did he want to see her again?

Touch her again, breathe in her scent, be with her again and feel her, naked, against him?

Well, yes. That was a definite yes.

But he'd never been in precisely this situation before.

Was Craig supposed to ask him about his intentions? Or maybe he was supposed to give Micah a good left hook to the jaw.

"You're sleeping with her, right?" Craig asked.

"Define sleeping," Micah said. "I only knew her as your cousin and a voice on the phone until two days ago. Last night, yes. We were together." He hesitated and then admitted. "I actually tried to leave. Probably not hard enough."

Craig lowered his head, obviously amused.

"Just keep her safe," he said.

And then, before either one of them could say any more, the phone in the conference room rang.

Craig picked it up and frowned as he listened to what was being said. He hung up slowly, rising as he did. "Come on, Egan's office. He's got a video call up with one of our agents in Cairo."

"Already? They have Satima Mahmoud?" Micah asked.

"No, but they have some kind of information," Craig replied.

They strode rapidly down the hall. Egan's secretary waved them in and they entered his office. He was speaking with someone via his computer; they both walked around behind his desk.

Micah had met the agent on the screen. His name was Sanford Wiley, and Micah quickly greeted him. Egan introduced him to Craig.

"So, we got your inquiry just now and I happened to be in the office," Wiley said. "I don't know whether it means anything or not, but I wanted to get back to you right away with what I have. The local police are looking for Satima Mahmoud. Now, they're not always entirely forthright with us, but from what I've been able to gather, she's suspected of having something to do with agitating trouble— and insurrection. She was under suspicion by the Egyptian police, who are now helping our people with the investigation, we believe, as well. They've been searching for her for several days. We'll start our own line of investigation, since she's a witness or person of interest to you all. Fox, I know you had some interaction with her. Do you suspect her of being involved in Henry Tomlinson's death?"

"When I saw her, she informed me that the others had left. She had just gotten to Cairo herself when I was trying to head out to the expedition site," Micah told him. "I'm very interested in what she may know. Or more specifically, what she knows that she didn't share at the time. She was the one who first sounded the alarm about the uprising. Everything was pure chaos when I was there, which I'm sure you remember, Wiley. But, yes, if you find her, I'd very much like to speak with her."

"We're on it from this end—with the Egyptian police, of course."

"Of course."

"We get the impression that they're perplexed about the situation. She's disappeared."

"Thanks for letting us know," Micah told him.

There were a few more exchanges, and then they ended the video call.

Egan looked thoughtfully at Micah. "To be honest," he said, "I'm not sure what you can learn from this woman—or what you could prove—this late in the game. Crews are still going through whatever evidence they could find at the museum after Vivian was attacked, but…"

"I know, sir," Micah said. "But it's only been a matter of days. And I'm pretty convinced that Vivian Richter's attack relates back to Henry's death. And if not, well, we still need to know who the hell would attempt to murder a woman with nicotine-soaked linen wrappings."

"Yes, and we *will* find the truth," Egan said with conviction. "I'll inform you of anything we learn through our people here and in Egypt, and through any chatter they pick up." He hesitated. "If they can't find this woman…"

"There's always the possibility that she's dead," Craig finished.

"Why kill an interpreter?" Egan mused.

"There's also the possibility that she's alive—and more of a player than we'd imagined," Micah said. "Or that very fact could account for her death. If that's what happened."

"When you talked to her, did you get the feeling that she was involved in any way?" Craig asked.

"She seemed harried, frightened and glad to be back in Cairo. But I was still trying to catch up with the Americans involved. Now I realize I should have given her more attention then. The entire situation was terrifying, so of course it seemed reasonable that she'd be upset. And I still don't see her with a motive of any kind to strangle Henry."

"You never know," Egan told him.

"Except we do know that she's definitely not in the States," Craig said. He suddenly began to feel his pocket, which was apparently vibrating. "Phone," he muttered. "Excuse me, two seconds. This may be important." He answered the call, taking a step back from Micah and Egan.

"She's not in this country that we know of, anyway," Micah said to Egan. He hesitated, speaking carefully. "I still don't think she killed Henry."

"But you think she might know who did?"

"I think she knows *something*," Micah said. "She's Joe Rosello's alibi for the time Jensen Morrow and Harley Frasier were away from the camp. What if she lied because he either cajoled her or bribed her?"

Egan nodded. "That's a possibility."

"You're talking about Joe Rosello?" Craig asked, putting away his phone.

"Yes," Micah said.

"That was Kieran. She's going to Times Square with Harley. And it's about Joe Rosello. The man's an actor, and he's in a zombie walk today. Not sure I actually get it, but Kieran knew about it because of her twin, Kevin. He's one of the performers hired on as an improvisational actor and guide for the walk."

"Sounds like a good time for us to get to Times Square and see just what he's up to," Micah said.

"Zombie walk?" Egan asked, shaking his head.

"They're all over the country now," Micah told him. "The power of television and mass media today. The popularity of certain television programs can create some strange circumstances."

"There's a show on TV about mummies?"

"Mummies, zombies, walking dead. Close enough, I think. Let's head on out," Micah said to Craig. "With your blessing, sir, of course," he added, addressing Egan.

"Go, sir, with righteousness!" Egan said. "And get the whacked-out son of a bitch, will you? Speaking of media—they're having a heyday with this. Mummies! As if we didn't have enough of the plain old walking, living, flesh-and-blood kind of criminals!"

A MAJORITY OF the "zombies" there for the walk and to support the charity were dressed up.

They wore zombie makeup, tattered clothing and many looked as if they'd rolled in the dirt.

Luckily, not all the participants were dressed up, and since it was a charity walk, whatever one chose to wear was fine. Joining the walk cost ten dollars. The fee included a comedy "zombie" performance at the end, with the bleachers reserved for those who'd paid. Anyone could see the show, but since the entry fee went to charity—three of the major children's hospitals—virtually no one was going to mind paying.

"This would've been fun no matter what," Kieran told Harley, surveying the crowd. "A lot of the costumes on the walkers are really cool. Oh, there, at the sign-up tables. There's Kevin."

Kieran started walking ahead; Harley quickly followed.

Kevin Finnegan was an exceptionally good-looking man, tall, with great bone structure, a toned body and broad shoulders. He and Kieran were clearly related, but of course, they weren't just siblings—they were twins. Like Kieran, he had deep auburn hair and his eyes were a true blue.

Harley waited while Kieran greeted her

brother with a hug and a kiss; she then greeted him, as well.

"I'm so glad you came out. I know how you feel about crowds in Times Square," Kevin told his sister.

"It's…well…" Kieran began.

"Ah. I'm being used," Kevin said, but his smile was affectionate. "What do you need? How can I help?"

"We signed up legitimately, don't you fear," Kieran said. "But do you know a Joe Rosello?"

"Not that I'm aware of."

"No? Oh, I guess you don't know everyone working here today," Harley said.

"Actually, I do."

"Oh! Well, supposedly, Joe's working."

"Maybe he works under a different name. SAG rules mean you can't use a name if someone else has it already. Or even if he's not SAG, he might be using a stage name," Kevin said.

"That's him! That's him right there!" Harley exclaimed.

"Oh, so that's your guy. His name is Robbie. At least when he's here it is. Nice guy, or so it seems."

Joe—or Robbie Rosello, as he was calling himself for the day—was standing over by one of the tables. As Kevin had been doing, he was posing with people who wanted their pictures taken with a zombie.

He was dressed in tatters. Not like a mummy, just in tatters. His skin was painted white and he had very effective makeup that darkened his eyes and made his cheeks sink in.

As Joe so often did, he was flirting.

"Yep, that's him!" Harley said again.

The girls with whom he'd been posing moved on, and Harley ran over to him. He turned to look at her and his eyes widened with surprise, alarm—and wariness.

"Harley!" he said. "Um, what are you doing here? You're a zombie fan?" He sounded skeptical.

"It's a good cause, right? You know, I was shocked to find out that you're an actor."

"Oh, well…" He smiled at her awkwardly. "I'm not really an actor, more of an 'I love the movies' kind of guy who likes to get work as an extra. I don't hide it, but I guess I don't talk about it at work. There are people who don't think you can be a serious academic if you…if you do things like take part in a zombie walk."

"That's silly."

"Yeah? Well, we both know the world can be full of silliness, some of it malicious."

She nodded. "I guess, but if this is something you love, you shouldn't have to be afraid that others won't approve."

He frowned. "I agree."

"I guess we have to work on convincing the rest of the world."

"The academic world, anyway. How did you even find out about this?"

"You remember Craig Frasier, my cousin? He's dating Kieran Finnegan. And her brother, Kevin, is an actor—"

"Kevin is a *serious* actor. He actually makes a living at it," Joe said. He grimaced. "I don't think I'd be able to do that, so I have to be a serious academic instead."

"By the way, you look great," she told him.

"Thank you."

"Is the costume yours? Do you have many… costumes?"

"Oh, no. No," he said firmly, apparently figuring out just where she was going with her question and why she was really there, "No! Emphatically no. I've never dressed up like a mummy." He hesitated. "I swear, I'd never have hurt Henry, and I did nothing to Vivian Richter. I swear!"

"Hey, Robbie! Zombie dance thing starting up," someone called.

"Excuse me, gotta go. Don't worry. I'll have

thousands of witnesses for my every move today," he assured Harley.

"Have fun!" she said.

He gave her a thumbs-up and joined a number of other actors, Kevin Finnegan among them. Someone struck a chord on a guitar, and the group went into a shuffle dance, akin to the one in the music video for Michael Jackson's old "Thriller."

The song was very clever, and the words had to do with giving generously to fight disease.

And when it was over, Kevin—the head zombie, apparently—stepped out from the group and announced they'd be walking down Broadway. Volunteers with water were positioned along the route. The walk would end at the bleachers, where some of the entertainers would then be performing.

Harley turned and looked around until she finally saw Kieran. Kieran saw her at the same time and hurried toward her as a sea of people—some in zombie rags and makeup, some not—came between them. They were almost carried along by the crowd. Kieran shrugged and waved at her from a distance, then laughed as they were both pushed along.

Harley tried to thread her way through the would-be zombies.

Kieran did the same.

Now and then, they'd come across another kind of creature, something from Disney or perhaps one of Jim Henson's characters from his movies or television shows.

Harley ran into some comic characters she didn't recognize. A man in a very large banana suit struggled to maneuver to the side.

He fell over.

She tried to reach him, but he was helped up by a group of grapes. Police were everywhere on the street and they also tried to help the banana; the grapes were just faster.

It was Times Square, after all.

And Times Square on an especially crazy day. It reminded her why she usually avoided the area. But a lot of the theaters were down here, too, and she did love going with Craig and Kieran to see plays when Kevin was in them—and even when he wasn't!

But today…

"Hey there!" Kieran called. She was walking parallel with Harley, a few feet to the left.

"Hey!" Harley called back, grinning.

But then she saw the mummy.

On a day like this, it was difficult to discern the differences between costumes; many were tattered white, and appeared to have been made from linen strips.

But this...

This was a mummy.

It was a mummy that looked exactly the way Vivian Richter had looked when she'd staggered into the midst of the gala. It might've been created by the same costume artist! Or would-be costume artist...

The thing was behind her, lurching along. Harley scanned the crowd. The mummy seemed to be walking alone.

And walking in a casual manner that brought it closer and closer to Harley.

"Kieran!" she screamed.

At first, her friend turned to her with a broad smile. Then she saw the mummy. And she began to stride aggressively over to Harley—with the mummy between them.

The mummy sensed pursuit and headed toward Kieran. But then, it headed back in Harley's direction with a purpose and a vengeance, no longer staggering.

"Come on, come on, I'm ready for you!" Harley thought. "Police! Police!" she cried.

And then the thing was upon her, placing a hand on her chest. It looked right at her, but she couldn't see its eyes. They were covered in the same linen gauze that stretched over the body, dirtied and rendered old, as if—mummy or zombie—the creature had long been dead.

THE THRONG OF people was impressive, particularly for a charity event.

Micah assumed many people were out just for the entertainment value and, of course, the fun of dressing up as a zombie.

But it made for a massive crowd—tens of thousands at the very least, and maybe many more considering the size of New York City.

"I see Kevin Finnegan," Craig said.

"Where?"

"Leading the zombie charge."

"You're sure that's Kevin?"

"Yes, and if so, Kieran is near him, and if she is…"

"Then Harley's near Kieran. Let's go!"

Wending their way through the horde of people wasn't easy. Apparently, no one had thought to tell the regular performers who thronged Times Square daily in costume, charging for tourist pictures, that zombies would be ruling the day.

Maybe it didn't matter. As they hurried past the Times Square Marriott, Micah saw a zombie posing with a Disney figure and with one of the imitation "naked" cowboys who'd staked a claim on the street.

He kept up a brisk pace, saying "excuse me" almost every other second.

And then he saw Kevin Finnegan, laughing, talking, making announcements through a speaker and pointing to the bleachers ahead.

He also saw Joe Rosello dancing along with a group as he moved forward in costume—ragged jeans, ripped rock band T-shirt and heavily made-up face and body.

And there...

A mummy!

A mummy, standing in the street, touching Harley, touching her with wrapped hands that appeared to be wet, soaked in something.

"Stop now!" he shouted.

He barely avoided knocking over a teenager playing zombie-on-a-crutch. In a circuitous route, he cleared a number of teens. As carefully as he could without losing speed, he continued to press forward through and around people.

The mummy saw him—and turned to run.

He heard Harley shout. She was starting to run after the thing.

"No!" He caught up with her.

"We have to catch that mummy!" she said.

"No, no—get your shirt off!"

"What?"

"Your shirt. Get your shirt off."

"Here? In Times Square?"

Craig, gasping for breath, had reached them. "Get your shirt off! The hands—the mummy's hands were covered in something. Get it off *now*. Harley, damn it, there could be poison on your shirt. Get it off before…"

She cried out, all but ripping the shirt from her body. It fell to the ground.

There were creatures of all kinds gathering around them.

"Way cool!" a passing zombie said.

"Yeah," said another. "It's legal, you know. Men can go topless, and women can go topless! New York City, man. What a great place."

"Maybe she'll take off her bra!"

"Moron!" Harley breathed, swinging around.

"I've got the shirt," Craig said, slipping into gloves and reaching down.

"The mummy's probably shedding poison with every step," Micah said. "Cops. Get cops over here. Warn them there's a hazard… gloves, bags…"

He didn't need to talk; Craig knew what had to be done as well as he did. Micah had already begun moving, and as he did, he swore. The "mummy" was indeed shedding, leaving what was likely poisoned and hazardous material every few steps.

But the trail of wrappings at least gave him a direction to take, as clear as tracking any animal, human included, in a forested wilderness.

"Look!" a girl cried. "It was a mummy! A mummy!"

She'd picked up some of the shredded linen that had been cast on the ground. Micah swore again, using his gloved hands to snatch it from her.

"Hey!" she protested.

"Get to a cop. Get to a doctor. That might be poisoned material," Micah said. A man quickly appeared at the child's side, holding her, and taking Micah more seriously than she did, apparently.

"Cop! Doctor!" Micah ordered.

"Yes, sir!" the man said, clutching his daughter.

Micah hurried on.

Cops were filling the area. Craig had gotten to Kevin Finnegan, and Kevin was announcing the problem, warning people not to touch the linen, to get to a cop, hospital, or doctor if they had.

Micah kept running. He saw more of the linen along the road. Swearing, he knew he'd have to stop and add it to the growing cache he stuffed into a large evidence bag as he hurried along.

The "mummy" had planned well, knowing that the police and FBI were fully aware that poison—using poisoned linen—was his or her talent.

And that they'd definitely be delayed in their pursuit, trying to keep others from becoming victims of possible illness or even death.

The last piece of linen was in front of an alley that led from Times Square down one of the side streets.

Micah swung around the corner, racing down the street. And then he stopped.

The street was filled with massive office buildings; there was also a massage place, a Chinese restaurant and somebody's bar and grill.

And there was no one on the street.

It was New York! Where was everyone?

But it was Sunday. Offices were closed. Whoever was getting a massage was already inside; any diners at the Chinese restaurant were already seated.

Micah hurried along the street. The mummy couldn't possibly have changed so quickly.

Or maybe it had. Maybe the linens had been shed completely and the mummy was just a normal person now, enjoying a delicious bowl of lo mein.

Micah moved on down the street.

Yeah, by now, the mummy might be just a "normal" person.

But Micah was sure it was going to be a normal person he knew. And he was determined to find that person. This time, he was chasing the damned mummy—person, whoever it was—to Jersey or Connecticut if he had to.

There! Up ahead.

The mummy was turning onto Fifth Avenue and heading north.

Micah started to run.

"Do you know who it was? Do you have any clue who it was?" Kieran asked Harley.

It had been a ridiculous, uncomfortable day. She was still half-naked, feeling embarrassed and exposed. Just because one *could* go topless according to NYC's equality laws, didn't mean she had any desire to do so! She was running through the crowd, Kieran keeping pace beside her, anxious to get to a car so she could go home and have a shower.

A taxi stopped for them when they made it over to Eighth Avenue. The driver grinned wolfishly at Harley, nodding when they gave him her address. A quick conversation with one of Craig's ME friends had assured them that Harley's going home for a shower would be fine; if the poison had touched only her clothing, there should be no problem, and of course, once the contaminated linen was analyzed, they'd know what they were looking at.

"We aren't even sure there *is* poison on the wrappings," Harley said.

"What do you want to bet?" Kieran asked her.

Harley didn't want to bet.

The mummy had taken her completely by surprise. She'd wanted to knock the thing in the head and rip the linen wrappings from it.

And instead…

It had touched her, and only Micah's arrival had kept her from contact with linen that was possibly doused in nicotine.

"How the hell is that damned mummy wearing poison and not dropping dead?" she demanded. The driver was staring back at her in his rearview mirror, even more interested than he'd been earlier. She leaned forward, ready to snap at him—and then didn't.

What the hell. She dropped back against the seat.

"Kieran, how is he or she doing it? All that poison?"

"Wearing something underneath the wrapping, I guess. We don't have anything analyzed yet, although I'm convinced that was actually an attempt on your life—or a warning for you to back off."

"Okay, so the mummy found me. But it looked as if the mummy was running through the crowd, touching anyone and everyone," Harley said.

"That was to stop the police or anyone in pursuit," Kieran told her.

"Hey!" Harley snapped. The taxi driver was grinning; he was about to take a roundabout route to her building. "No, go straight and then turn right!" she said.

"One-way street," the driver said in a singsong voice.

"And it's going the way we want it to!"

They reached their destination and Kieran paid the cabbie as they stepped out; Harley realized she was being rude.

"I'm sorry. Didn't mean to make you pay that!"

"Harley, that's the least of our concerns at the moment," Kieran said.

"They haven't called? Micah or Craig?"

"Harley, Micah was in hot pursuit and Craig was headed in to get those wrappings to the lab. It takes time. We're here. Listen, just smile at the clerk or security guy on duty," Kieran advised. "He's staring at you just like the taxi driver was. Now let's get up to your place."

Harley did manage a nice smile for the security guard on duty. He was staring at her, as Kieran had said, but at the last minute sent her a confused smile in return.

Upstairs, Harley told Kieran to make herself comfortable, and Kieran said she would. Harley showered.

And showered, nearly scrubbing herself raw in the process.

She emerged from the shower, wrapped in a robe, and hurried downstairs.

Kieran was on the phone. She turned to look at Harley.

"Good call on Micah's part. Yes, those wrappings were soaked in nicotine.

There was something odd about the way she was speaking.

"What is it?"

"Micah followed the mummy on foot—all the way up to Central Park and the museum."

"The New Museum of Antiquity?" Harley said.

"Yes. And he found a mummy...half-dead."

"Mummies *are* dead."

"No, I mean... I'm sorry, Harley. Arlo Hampton is probably going to die. He was found on the floor, stretched out in wrappings, right in front of the Temple of Ra."

Chapter Seven

The same day Vivian Richter was released from the hospital, Arlo Hampton was rushed in, swiftly ripped out of torn swaths of mummy wrappings.

This whole thing was his fault, or so it appeared.

He was both the would-be killer—and his own victim, in the end.

At least, Harley thought, that was how it appeared. Or how it was *supposed* to appear.

It seemed evident that he'd dressed up as a mummy but carefully gloved his hands in plastic before soaking a number of loose and shredded strips of "decayed" linen in nicotine and then heading out to assault a "zombie" crowd. Afterward he'd returned to the museum, only to collapse there.

Perhaps he had started back in the Sahara. Perhaps his jealousy, his determination to rise in his field, had caused him to attack Henry Tomlinson back at the expedition prep tent. He must have attacked Vivian as a mummy. She'd blacked out and he had dressed her up and when she came to, he'd sent her, crazed, into the crowd, where she'd been saved.

Today...

No one really knew his intent. Had he just meant to poison a bunch of random "zombies"? Had he known, perhaps, that Joe Rosello was going to be among the actors? Had he thought Joe knew something and needed to be silenced?

He'd come up to Harley.

He had touched her with his poisoned linen rags.

But he couldn't have known Harley would be there; Harley hadn't even known that herself until the last minute. That seemed to make Joe the chosen target.

Unless, of course, Arlo Hampton had just wanted to indiscriminately poison people in the crowd. None of them could determine the truth as yet. And if Arlo died, they might never find out.

Arlo might be accused of killing Henry, or the attempted murder of Vivian—and intent to attack Joe Rosello and a number of innocent "zombies" in the crowd. But he'd calculated wrong; he hadn't taken the right care. He had not been immune to the poison he'd been trying to administer to others.

They knew this, because Craig gave them whatever information he could over the phone. He and Micah had managed to get to the museum quickly; in fact, Micah had reached it just minutes after everything happened. He'd pursued the mummy from Times Square!

Harley insisted that she and Kieran needed to get to the museum.

She didn't know why; she just knew the whole thing simply didn't feel right.

They got there fairly fast. Officers in uniform were maintaining crowd control—the entire museum had been closed down—but someone on duty recognized Kieran. Craig was summoned, and the two of them were let through with Craig leading the way past more officers, spectators, and a sea of media at the entry.

Arlo Hampton no longer there, of course; he'd been rushed to the hospital. Photographers and crime scene technicians were still at work. Apparently, Arlo had been discovered by a pair of teenage girls who remained in a corner of the room, huddled together. They were still in shock. According to them, Arlo had grunted and tried to reach for them when they'd first found him, nearly giving them joint heart attacks. They'd now told their story a few times and were waiting for their parents.

Rydell and McGrady were there; it remained, after all, a joint investigation. They were with Craig and Micah, trying to create rational scenarios as to what might have happened.

Micah was looking at crime scene photos on his phone, photos snapped by the security guard first on the scene.

McGrady tried to stop Harley when she stepped forward to reach Micah.

"Ms. Frasier, I'm sorry, but you're in the way."

Micah immediately came to her defense. "She's got more degrees in criminology than the rest of us put together. She knew Arlo. She was stalked by him earlier and he tried to get to her at the zombie walk. Ms. Frasier may have something useful to say."

"What's there to say?" McGrady muttered. "He's probably going to die. We weren't there to get him to a hospital fast enough. Nicotine poisoning. Doc just said so—it's all over the wrappings. Jerk dressed up as a mummy for that damned zombie walk, and now he's dead by his own hand."

"It's not him," Harley said.

"What?" McGrady spun on her.

"That's not him—"

"Harley, it *is* Arlo Hampton," Craig interrupted, his tone firm as he frowned at her.

"Yes, Micah, I know Arlo's the one who was found here, but that's not the mummy who was at the zombie walk."

"Harley," Micah said slowly, "trust me. I've been running after him. Olympic-style running. I saw him when he turned north on Fifth. I followed this mummy from the zombie walk, and then I followed him down a bunch of streets, and I saw him go through the tunnel entrance to the museum. By the time I got through the maze down there and back up to the exhibit, those two teenagers were screaming." He was quiet for a minute. "Harley, it *had* to be him. We can't find any other mummies in the museum."

Harley blinked, looking at him.

"Yes, sorry, I know," Craig said, sounding aggravated and weary. "The museum's full of mummies. I mean living mummies. Living people dressed up as mummies. This place is crawling with security and we—"

"You're being an ass!"

He winced, and quickly apologized. "Yeah, sorry. I just don't see—"

"There are so many rooms and tunnels, and I'm telling you, this isn't the same mummy."

"What's different?" Craig asked her.

She didn't know! She couldn't tell. Judging by the photographs Craig and Micah had shown them, the wrappings appeared the same. True, the mummy walking through the crowd had been stripping off pieces of his wrapping, but that wasn't what bothered her, since Arlo's wrappings looked quite disheveled.

Somehow, this mummy—the mummy in the pictures, the Arlo Hampton mummy—was different. Not the wrappings so much, but…something.

"You think the cops are incompetent, Ms. Frasier?" McGrady turned his back on her.

Rydell shrugged apologetically.

"No, Detective, I think the cops are great. I've worked with lots of cops, including some of the ones here right now. Like I told you, I think they're great. You're not great. You've got a chip on your shoulder a mile wide."

"Harley," Micah said quietly.

"He's not just being patronizing and rude, he's jeopardizing an investigation!"

"Yes, that's true, but for the moment…"

"We're lead on this," Craig said.

"We need to start another search!" Micah announced, his voice booming.

"This is going to be reported," McGrady threatened.

"You bet," Micah promised him.

"Rydell, you saw it all."

"Yeah, I did," Rydell said.

Furious, McGrady stomped off. He seemed to be heading for the exit.

"Sorry," Harley murmured.

"No, you were in the right," Micah assured her. "Someone find me a blueprint of this place. Let's get on it. Every room, every display, every office. It's going to be a long day, folks. We're going to have to get down to the basement and below. Search everywhere."

A man in one of the crime scene jumpsuits approached Micah and Craig; they spoke for several minutes, and then a group of people in crime scene jumpsuits began to emerge from various corners of the exhibit. They were given instructions and dispersed, everyone going in a different direction.

"Micah?" Harley asked. "May I go to the museum lab? I'd like to see what's been going on there. I swear to you, I'm not sure how I know, but I'm convinced that the mummy who confronted me in the street didn't look the same as those pictures of Arlo. Maybe I can find something in the lab."

"I'll keep her company," Kieran volunteered.

"All right. I'll inform the crime scene people," Micah told them. "I'm going down below. Arlo was the one who showed us all the basement tunnels and entrances and exits." He watched Harley as he spoke. She wondered if he believed her; he'd stood with her against McGrady, who was being such a jerk, but she had to wonder…

Just how many mummies could there be running around?

Living mummies, rather than the dead ones.

Micah turned away and spoke with the crime scene people again. She noticed that Detective Rydell hadn't gone with his partner; he was awaiting a discussion with Craig and Micah.

"Come on through. We're going to be searching the offices," one of the crime scene women told Harley and Kieran. "Just follow us."

As they left the exhibit space behind and came into an employee hallway, Harley saw that Gordon Vincent, director of the museum, was arguing with the crime scene people. He looked at Harley with annoyance and then pointed at her. "This whole exhibit has turned into a disaster."

Harley looked back at him, startled. "Mr. Vincent, I'm sorry you feel that way. I don't think the exhibit can be blamed for what this person's doing. The artifacts that were discovered are amazing, sir, and law enforcement will get to the bottom of this."

Kieran stepped forward, offering Vincent a hand, "How do you do, sir? We haven't actually met. I'm Kieran Finnegan, a psychologist with the offices of Fuller and Mira. They're psychiatrists who spend a great deal of time working with law enforcement. From my field of study, I'd guess that—sad though it is— these horrible events won't hurt your museum. On the contrary—this will cause an influx of membership and tourism. People love mummies…and mysteries. You're receiving unbelievable media attention, and while these days may be hard to weather, I believe that in the end you'll find that the museum itself is in an excellent position, no matter how discouraging a comment that might be on humanity."

Vincent turned to Kieran, blinking. "Fine. It's all closed for the day. Make sure the powers that be within the FBI and NYPD let me know if I can or cannot open my museum in all or part tomorrow!"

He strode on by them.

Harley looked at Kieran and laughed. "I'm not even sure what you said myself!"

"It worked, though. I guess that's what matters."

"You were excellent."

"You can be more excellent in this situation. You're so involved. You need to really think about the people who are connected to the exhibit, and how and why they might be acting a certain way. You know all the players, Harley, and you have to think about every one of them."

"Well," Harley said, "I guess we can let Joe Rosello off the hook. I'm almost positive that he was the intended victim today. But then I happened to be there. And who knows what was really planned, since—"

"Harley, are you absolutely sure that Arlo Hampton wasn't the 'mummy' who came up to you at the zombie walk?"

"Kieran, I'm telling you, it wasn't him. And remember, Vivian Richter said a mummy came to her, and then, apparently, that mummy dressed her up as a mummy, too, in poisoned linen."

"I know," Kieran said. "But—"

"But that's the point, right? Vivian Richter was working in her office. A mummy came in and suddenly she's a mummy. Isn't it possible that the same thing happened today?"

"Of course," Kieran said. "But everyone's been searching...and they haven't found the stash of nicotine that's being used."

They reached the lab and walked through the outer entry; there were paper gowns and caps and booties to be worn inside the room.

"Really? Do we have to do all this?" Kieran muttered.

Harley laughed. "Yes! It helps prevent the spread of anything, any bacteria, that might be on antique, long-buried objects from getting out into the world. And it keeps us from bringing in anything that might be harmful to very old stuff."

"Okay, makes sense," Kieran said grudgingly.

"What I really want to do is get to Arlo's desk over there. The small one. See?"

Kieran nodded and followed Harley's actions as she suited up, donned gloves and booties, and then headed into the actual lab.

"What bothers me about this is the lack of clear motive," Kieran said. "It should be obvious, right in front of our faces. These people are dedicated to their work. It means as much to them as anything else in their lives. Maybe more. Most of us live for our mate, spouse, and so on, first—or our children. The instinct to protect a child is strong, except when you're talking about a person who's truly mentally impaired. But in our type of science, in psychiatry and criminology, you come across people who are more devoted to their work than to family or friends."

"Yes, and we think someone was terribly jealous of Henry—which is why he was killed. Now it seems that someone is trying to kill Vivian and Arlo—who are also hardworking and respected members of the Egyptology community. But…"

"But what?"

"I know I keep saying this, but I don't believe that Arlo and the mummy on the street were the same person. I just don't believe it. And Arlo was the one to walk Micah and me all around this place the other day. Do you think…?"

"Think what?"

"There's another motive? There's something we're missing?"

"Of course. That's always possible."

"Love, hate, greed, jealousy. Vengeance," Harley murmured.

"Ah, vengeance. For what? And against whom?"

Harley made her way to the small aluminum desk in the far corner of the room. It was made so it could be constantly sterilized, but still allow for a notepad, pens, tablet, computer or whatever else the scientists and lab techs might need to accurately notate their work.

She opened the first drawer, which held a large plastic container of sanitary wipes.

She opened the second drawer. There was an unused notepad and a case of pencils.

There should've been a computer somewhere. A tablet. Even a voice recorder.

There was not.

Harley opened the third drawer. And there she saw, shoved against the back, a small, almost archaic, flip phone.

She pulled it out and studied it carefully. It had the look of a phone that might be bought at any convenience or drug store—pay as you go. She hit key after key; nothing on it denoted ownership. She went to contacts.

Her own number was there, along with the numbers of others who'd been on the expedition.

"Kieran," she said slowly.

"You found something?"

Harley looked up at her. "Maybe. I think I may just have found a way to reach our liaison, Yolanda, who hasn't been seen since the night of the party. And I think we might have a connection to our long-missing interpreter, Satima Mahmoud."

"In 1524, New York was called New Angoulême by the Italian explorer Giovanni da Verràzzano," Micah said to Craig as they traveled deep into the underbelly of the museum. "The first recorded exploration by the Dutch was in 1609. In 1664, English frigates arrived and demanded the surrender of the city. Peter Stuyvesant sent lawyers to arrange the capitulation—the Dutch and the English liked to go at it in those days. Well, come to think of it, over the years most European powers went after one another. Anyway, it was in 1665 that the city became New York under English rule."

"A lecture on New York history while we're looking for mummies—which happen to be a good bit older than the city," Craig said.

"True, but my point is that although it's not old in comparison with some cities in Africa, the Middle East, the Far East and Europe, New York *is* old. And while it all started downtown—Wall Street, Broad Street and so on—it's been many years since people came up to this area by subway. And down here in these tunnels, especially with so many routes now abandoned, it's just a jungle."

"Yep. And hey, love my city and all…but you just gave away the fact that you were some mean historian before you were a special agent."

"Actually, I'm complaining. This is like looking for a needle in a haystack," Micah said, and he sighed, leaning back against a wall to catch his breath.

He nearly fell backward.

"What the hell?"

"Hey!"

Craig made a grab for Micah's arm; Micah caught hold of him just in time to keep from plunging through a decayed section of wall.

They both half fell and half stumbled into the remains of an old subway tunnel.

The posters on the walls were peeling, but they were magnificent; they advertised Broadway shows opening in the 1930s. There were stairways to nowhere crafted of wrought iron and beautifully designed.

"There!" Micah said, gesturing with one hand at something extremely modern that marred the time-travel look of the place.

In a corner where plaster and paneling had decayed with time, there was a pile of insecticide containers.

At least fifty of them.

Enough poison to kill… God alone knew how many people.

"THERE HAS TO be some evidence there, right? *Something?*" Harley asked anxiously.

She was seated at a corner table at Finnegan's, along with Micah, Craig and Kieran. Crime scene crews had gone into the offshoot of the abandoned subway station, and they were studying every piece of evidence—primarily the containers of insecticide—with every technique available to them to find out who had used them. Or at least where and when they'd been purchased.

No one had answered when they'd tried to reach Yolanda Akeem or Satima Mahmoud; Egan had people working the phones as well, trying to find a way to pin down the locations of the women's phones via the contact information.

Now it was a matter of waiting.

And it was still Sunday. Although it was late, they had friends in the kitchen, so they were able to enjoy Sunday's traditional roast.

"Here's the thing. We've known that Yolanda Akeem was here in New York. She was at the museum when everything happened with Vivian," Harley said. "And after they questioned her briefly, she left."

"She was visible on security footage," Micah reminded her.

"I think we definitely have a problem, and everyone's part of it—the museum and the Egyptian Department of Antiquities, as well as our government and their government," Craig said. "The truth was left to slide."

"Murder is ugly. No one wants a part of it," Micah murmured to Harley.

"Were any artifacts stolen?" Kieran asked.

"No. Not that I know of," Harley replied. "And what about the motives for any of this? Jealousy, as we already discussed? I keep thinking that a longing for glory seems obvious. Too obvious? The people who would've been jealous of Henry were Arlo and Vivian—and they were the ones who were attacked."

"And you don't think I was an intended victim?" Joe Rosello asked. "Rather than you?"

Harley looked up and smiled. Joe and Kevin had arrived together, all cleaned up and out of their zombie makeup.

Micah and Craig had risen; Kevin brought a couple of extra chairs to draw up to their table and then left telling Joe he was going to arrange for two more meals.

"You *were* an intended victim," Micah told Joe flatly. "Had to be. The culprit couldn't have known that Harley was going to be there. Harley didn't know it herself until she talked to Kieran and found out about the zombie walk and that *you'd* be there."

"But…we should be safe, shouldn't we? I heard Arlo was the culprit and that he's in the hospital—and they don't know if they can save him or not."

"It's true that Arlo is in the hospital. And many people believe he was the mummy and that he was guilty of trying to kill Vivian. She did, after all, say that a mummy had come to her."

"Was there time for the mummy to have reached the museum and attacked someone else to create a new mummy?" Kieran asked.

"You did say that you were right behind him, getting to the museum," Harley said.

"I'm afraid that yes, there was time. I followed the mummy, but I was still some distance away when I saw him go down to the basement area of the museum. Then, of course, I stumbled around down there myself for a while. They need to wall all of that off, because if they don't, they're going to lose some curious fifth-grader down there one day."

"I'm taking a leave from my job," Joe said. "I'm getting out of here tomorrow morning. When this is all over, I'll come back. I called the museum I'm working at and they understood."

"That might be your best move," Micah told him.

Joe let out a long sigh. "Thank God! I thought you were going to tell me I wasn't allowed to leave town."

"We'll need your contact information. However, you were in full sight of thousands of people most of the day. It would be very hard to prove you had any involvement," Craig said.

"Thank God," he muttered again.

Kevin Finnegan returned to the table. The talk shifted back and forth between the zombie walk and the situation at the museum.

Suddenly they all seemed to realize it had grown very late.

"I'm going home so I can get out of here in the morning," Joe said. "You all take care."

"We need to know where you'll be and how to reach you," Craig said.

"You bet. Just no sharing anything that's gone on," Joe said.

"No sharing," they all swore at once.

"I take it you're getting Harley home?" Craig asked Micah.

Kieran looked at Harley—who refused to look back at her.

She didn't know. *Was* he seeing her home? She'd thrown herself at him last night; maybe he'd changed his mind about her during the very long day.

"Yes, I'll make sure she gets home safely," Micah said. He managed to keep a straight face. Harley was surprised that he could.

Actually, she was surprised that she didn't flush. She just smiled sweetly at Kieran, who was obviously amused, intrigued and, Harley hoped, glad that she and Micah seemed to be getting on very well, indeed.

As he drove her home, there was so much to say; so much speculation in which they could indulge.

But they didn't talk at all.

The minute they reached Harley's place and closed the door to her apartment, they were in each other's arms. Micah impatiently shed his Glock first; Harley shrugged out of her jacket, grabbing for his shirt as she tore at her own buttons.

Micah drew the shirt over her head before she could get to the last of the buttons. She had her hands on his waistband and his belt buckle, while their lips merged in a deep and fiery kiss that was also sweet and breathless and filled with laughter.

There was a fair amount of awkwardness that went along with stripping so quickly, with wanting nothing more than to touch, to feel, to kiss…

Clothing wound up strewn all over the floor.

Harley hoped there was no one on the street as she raced past the windows and headed for the stairway.

Micah caught up with her. He swept her into his arms.

"Oh, no! You can't…they're winding stairs. We'll end up—"

"I can do it this way!" he assured her, tossing her over his shoulder.

And he could. He made it up the winding stairway. Dropped her naked on the bed and fell beside her. Still panting, he raised himself on one elbow.

Harley pushed him back down.

She rained kisses over his naked body, reaching all around, taking him into her mouth.

He lifted her up, pulled her to him, rolled with her, kissed and teased and took his kisses everywhere until she cried out. They kissed and laughed in the tangled sheets, and then they were locked together again and the laughter was gone. They were too breathless, too desperate…

This was new. So new. It had been a long time since she'd chanced a relationship with anyone. It was wonderful because…

Because it was wonderful.

She knew with an indefinable certainty that it would always be good with him. They were so easy together. They could laugh, even do silly things, and those things somehow became erotic. She wanted to forget the world and curl up next to him forever, except that one could never really forget the world.

And, of course, that was it.

She could be with him—as if he were an oasis— and still talk about the burning sands and the desert around them. She could make love, hot and wickedly wet and exciting—and she could still tell him what she was thinking. They could share confidences and exchange opinions without any risk of betrayal.

She was in lust…and maybe falling in love.

"She knows something," Micah was saying. "I'm sure she does."

"She? Which she? Vivian, Belinda, Yolanda or Satima?" Harley asked. She propped herself up on an elbow to look down at him.

"Satima. I mean Satima," he said. "As for Yolanda, I think she just wants to keep her nose clean. She hates it that something connected to the Department of Antiquities has negative baggage attached to it. I'd swear she just doesn't want to get involved with the ugliness of it. Egan is working the diplomatic channel to get her to come and talk to us. As far as we can tell, she's still in the States. She may not have anything for us, but I'd still love to talk to her myself."

"McGrady could have turned her off American law enforcement forever and ever," Harley said.

"Sad thing is, he might have been a decent cop. You don't get to be a detective unless you come up through the ranks or know someone. He has no patience."

"And no ability with people," Harley put in.

Micah shrugged. "I want to talk to the missing girl, Satima, as well. And now we have a number for her that we didn't have before—thanks to you knowing where to dig. So to speak."

"Ah, yes…dig. The crime scene people would've found that phone. I don't know why Arlo had it where he did—or why he thought he needed a special phone."

"It's a chip phone, good around the world. Maybe that was the intent," Micah suggested. He sighed, bringing her closer. "I keep feeling we're looking at a giant puzzle and we should be able to see what it is, what the whole picture represents. Except there's one piece missing. If only we had that piece."

"We will have that piece," Harley said confidently. "You and Craig, the FBI, NYPD. You'll find that piece. It's like…"

Her voice trailed off.

"Like?"

"Well, you know my main role in the expedition was to find more clues as to what might have happened to Amenmose. He was murdered. He was buried hastily by someone who loved him. There are many suspects, of course. He was a threat to Ay, who was regent for Tut, and who did become pharaoh in his own right. He was also despised by Tut's sister and brother-in-law. But nothing I've found in any of the ancient stories or records suggests that one of those people killed him. He had a family, and servants, so I guess the suspects are endless. I feel the same way about that as you do—as we both do—about our current case. Suspects everywhere, but it seems impossible to get the real motive pinned down. Or to determine the whereabouts of each suspect at the crucial times."

"Process of elimination," Micah said. "Joe Rosello. People did see him all day long."

"Vivian Richter. She got out of the hospital late that morning."

"I'd still like to find out if she was home the rest of the day!"

"But…"

"Something might occur to her," Micah said.

"Everyone, including you, seems to believe that Arlo Hampton is guilty. That he poisoned himself trying to poison others."

"Hey, I keep an open mind! You say the mummy who touched you on the street was someone different. I believe you."

"We don't know where Jensen Morrow was today. Or Belinda."

"Or—at this moment—Vivian or Ned Richter. Or Roger Eastman. But we'll know soon."

"We will?"

He smiled at her. "Of course. Craig and I are just cogs in a giant machine, a machine that doesn't stop. Anyway, I agree with you. Something still isn't right. First thing I want is a conversation with Satima Mahmoud. Then Ned and Vivian Richter. Then…"

"It's about motive," Harley said.

"Motive," he repeated.

He was done talking.

He pulled her back into his arms.

And she lost herself in the feel of him against her.

Chapter Eight

Micah woke to the sound of his phone ringing—somewhere.

He remembered that he'd shed his clothing downstairs.

He leaped out of bed and hurried down the winding wrought iron staircase, glancing at the picture windows that looked out over the night, the city and Grace Church.

He sped across the room, thinking they had to remember to buy drapes—major drapes—before night fell again. Of course, that was being presumptuous, but…

He couldn't force his thoughts in any other direction.

His phone. He dived for his jacket and caught it on the eighth ring.

"Fox."

"Fox!" It was Richard Egan. "We have Yolanda Akeem down here. She's going to be returning to Egypt later this morning. She's with a friend of mine from the State Department. I suggest you get in quickly. I'll inform Frasier, too."

"Yes, sir!"

Micah turned off the phone and ran around finding the rest of his clothing. He tore up the stairs.

Harley was sleepily beginning to rise.

"What is it?" she asked anxiously. "It's not even seven," she murmured. "I guess that's not so early."

"I have to go. Now. They've got Yolanda down at the FBI office. She's leaving for Egypt, and she's with someone from the State Department."

"Go!"

He ran for the shower. She didn't follow him.

They both knew why that wouldn't be a good idea.

In a few minutes he was dressed and heading for the stairs. Harley had slipped into a robe to accompany him down. "We should've set coffee to brew last night," she murmured, opening the door so he could leave.

He paused to kiss her quickly on the lips.

"We weren't thinking about coffee. Personally, I'd forgo the coffee for what we did last night. I'll call you as soon as I know anything. You're not working today, are you?"

"No, nothing for Fillmore," Harley said. "Maybe I'll hang around and read for a while."

"Sounds good. Talk soon," he promised.

Then he was out the door. The office wasn't far, and once there, he could leave the car with a young agent in the street. No more than thirty minutes had passed since he'd answered his phone to Egan, but he couldn't help being a little afraid Yolanda might already have left.

She was returning home; this was his chance.

To his great relief, she was there. He learned from the receptionist that Egan was with her in the conference room. He hurried there— just in time to fall in step with Craig Frasier, who'd arrived, as well.

"Think she has anything?" Craig asked hopefully.

"Your guess is as good as mine." Micah shrugged. "But anything she does have might be worthwhile."

"Too true, when we keep stumbling in the dark. Literally. In the basement and below at the museum."

"Someone knows the museum—and knows it well."

They'd reached the conference room.

When they entered, Egan and the handsomely dressed man who had accompanied Yolanda Akeem rose to meet them. Yolanda started to rise; they quickly urged her to remain seated.

"Gentlemen, Ms. Yolanda Akeem and Mr. Tom Duffy from the State Department," Egan said. "Special Agents Craig Frasier and Micah Fox."

Everyone sat then.

"Thank you for being here," Micah told Yolanda. "We know you don't have to speak with us. We're grateful that you're willing to do so."

Yolanda Akeem was an attractive woman, probably approaching fifty. Her eyes and skin were dark, a testament to a rich and diverse background. Her appearance was dignified, almost regal.

She nodded. "I would have spoken earlier, if I'd thought I had something of value to say," she said. She wrinkled her nose. "I spoke with that silly policeman when Vivian Richter was attacked. He wanted to know if I believed that mummies could come to life—if I thought that curses were real! They *are* real, of course, when we are cursed with foolish people!"

"We weren't in charge of the investigation then, Ms. Akeem," Egan said.

"Yes, I know. And I spoke with Special Agent Fox before, when we were both reeling from the loss of a dear friend." Yolanda Akeem looked over at Micah and smiled sadly. "So, so sad. So much trouble. Such a terrible time."

"Yes, a terrible time," Micah agreed.

Yolanda waved a hand in the air. "Everyone running and rushing—and Henry barely cold. And then, of course—the insurrection! Children mewling that they are not privileged enough. A mountain out of a molehill. But... safety first, always. Yes, it's a tough world and there are very real terrors and threats. But in this case..."

"Yes."

"My friend, Special Agent Fox, believes that something about this entire situation, and about the tentative conclusions we've managed to reach, isn't right," Craig said. "Frankly, we may be looking too hard at the wrong suspects."

Yolanda Akeem hesitated. "I wish I could say, 'No, you're wrong.' But, you see, there's a bad taste in my mouth, although I don't understand why. The expedition was going well, or at least I thought so. Henry had worked in my country many times before. We loved him. And his students…they were charming. I was happy to work with them, too. The people from Alchemy…well, I overheard them having arguments with each other over money now and then. How much was being spent, where they needed to save. Of course, it was funny because Mr. Richter was the on-site CEO for the company and he was watching pennies, while his wife… She's a true dreamer and scientist, I believe. Money meant nothing to her." She grinned. "Henry ignored them all. Arlo Hampton tried to remind everyone that *he* was the main Egyptologist for Alchemy. Still, despite the little spats, it all seemed to be going well enough. But then… Henry died."

"You were at the camp that night?"

"I was. Belinda was going to go into town with Harley and Jensen, but she's engaged, you know. They will marry soon, I hope. Video chatting with her fiancé was a highlight for both of them. Belinda used my equipment for her chats. I was doing paperwork, and she was with me."

Micah glanced at Craig. It seemed that they could definitely scratch Belinda off any list that had to do with Henry's death.

"But you saw Henry."

"I saw Henry. Just for a few minutes early in the evening. I also saw our young inter-

preter, Satima Mahmoud, with Mr. Rosello.
Joe, yes, Joe Rosello."

Micah nodded. Joe was already off their
list. He'd been on the zombie walk—and he'd
been costumed as a zombie, not a mummy.

He couldn't believe he was even thinking
that way!

Yolanda suddenly frowned. "Perhaps trouble was in the air. I heard Satima arguing
with Joe. They didn't usually argue. They
were beautiful people, you know? Both of
them. But that night Satima was tired. She
just wanted to go home. Joe kept saying that
he wanted to finish the work. She said the
work wouldn't go away, and she had family
she had to see. So it was...a hot, troubled evening. Yes, hot in the desert, of course. But
the Richter husband and wife were arguing,
and Satima and Joe were arguing. Henry was
busy with his new treasures. Arlo wanted a
bigger role, and I think he saw Henry as a
means to that end, but he knew he had to leave
him at some time. He was testy... That evening I wanted nothing more to do with any
of them. Satima was...almost nasty to me! If
I'd hired her, I would have fired her right then
and there. I speak many languages. My father
was Egyptian, but my mother was Mexican

and French. I can interpret nicely. I wish I'd been the one doing that job."

She looked at them all and released a long breath.

"I will admit that I wasn't crazy about Vivian Richter, but I'm sorry she was hurt. Arlo... I'm sorry he was hurt, too. After Henry's death, he got his own way with Alchemy and the exhibit, but he did not seem like a bad person. Did he do all this? Why? For position? For glory? They say that he is going to die, most likely. He was not found as quickly as Vivian."

"We don't know if he was guilty," Egan said. "Or if he was a victim."

Yolanda shook her head. "I'm sorry. I know nothing more. And I did not mean to be... unhelpful. You may feel free to call me with more questions if you wish. I am returning to Cairo, but I will be accessible to you, if I can be of any more help."

Everyone rose, bidding one another goodbye.

Then the man from the State Department and the Egyptian liaison were gone. Egan, Craig and Micah were left to look at one another.

"This is the first I've heard of everyone fighting," Micah said. "Even when I was in

Cairo, it didn't come up. Of course, everything was chaos then."

"That could explain," Craig began, "why Ned Richter wasn't sitting at his wife's side the entire time she was in the hospital. If they'd been fighting, I mean."

"And maybe he wasn't with her yesterday," Egan said. "Check into it. And also, we've got people hot on the trail of the interpreter, Satima Mahmoud. Let's hope they'll be able to find her. They work hard at keeping up good communications with the police, here and abroad."

"What about Arlo Hampton?" Micah asked. "Anything? He made it through the night?"

"He's alive, yes, hanging on. Unconscious," Egan said. "Doctors... Well, I'm used to speaking with medical examiners. Seems I understand them a lot better than the guys who treat the living. Anyway, Arlo Hampton's still alive but they're not sure about neurological impact."

"The guy could end up a vegetable," Craig said.

"He could pull through all the way. They had to put him in a medically induced coma. When they bring him out of that, we might learn something. Anyway, he's alive, but he's sure as hell not going to be working soon," Egan said.

"Let's trust that he makes it," Micah said quietly.

"I guess maybe we should try speaking with Ned Richter and Joe Rosello again," Craig said.

"Rosello came out squeaky clean," Egan reminded them.

"Yes, but I don't think our missing interpreter is so squeaky clean," Micah said.

"You really think this Egyptian woman—who isn't even in this country—is involved?" Egan asked, puzzled.

"Yes. But I haven't figured out how. She can't be found. I'm hoping that doesn't mean she's dead," Micah said.

"Joe wasn't playing a mummy yesterday. We know that. But I agree with Micah," Craig said. "It'll be interesting as hell to find out what was going on between him and Satima Mahmoud."

"I'M SO SORRY. You sound terribly depressed," Harley told Jensen.

He'd called early, right around eight. Of course, by eight, half of New York was already bustling, but with no real plans, Harley had actually thought she'd be able to sleep in.

And simply enjoy the fact that she lay in sheets where they'd been together, where Micah's scent still lingered.

But she was glad to hear from Jensen; he was still trying to function, despite all else.

"Well, of course, I'm depressed," Jensen Morrow said over the phone. "Cops all over the place. It's necessary, I guess. Vivian came around fast—got better, survived!—but I understand Arlo's in bad shape. On the other hand, if Arlo did kill Henry and tried to kill Viv, he deserves whatever's happening to him."

"I don't think he did it, Jensen. He didn't commit any crimes yesterday, at any rate. I saw the mummy in the street, or *a* mummy in the street, and—"

She broke off. She suddenly knew what had been different about the mummy in the street and the pictures of Arlo Hampton as a mummy, passed out, almost dead, on the museum floor.

She wasn't sure it would be wise to share that information with anyone other than Micah, Craig and the police.

Jensen didn't seem to notice that she'd abruptly stopped speaking. "I'm here at work," he continued. "Let's see, Ned Richter is due in, and—you're not going to believe this!—Vivian Richter is coming with him. She's barely out of the hospital. She may be a bitch on wheels, but she's a trouper, I'll give her that. The woman loves her Egyptology! Needless to say, Arlo won't be here. And it's lonely without him. None of our buds are around. Belinda and Roger are busy with their own work. Talked to Joe—he left town this morning. He's scared. He thinks the mummy in the crowd was after him. And that might be true. Who knows? But if the mummy *was* Arlo, then none of us has anything to worry about. Right?"

The mummy in the street had not been Arlo Hampton. Arlo was tall. The mummy hadn't been very tall.

"Jensen, I don't think Arlo was guilty of anything."

"Some criminologist you are! You want to believe the best about everyone," Jensen muttered. "Are you going to come in and keep me company and help me ward off mummies?" he asked.

"I—I was going to spend some time with Craig's girlfriend."

"The lovely Kieran. So the two of you are going to dig deep into all our minds and figure out which one of us is the sicko? Whoever it is has to be crazy as a bat. I can see the defense in court. 'The bacteria made me do it!'"

Harley couldn't help smiling. "Defense attorneys. It's their job. But, yes, bacteria. It can affect the mind."

"Should I leave town?" Jensen asked her seriously. "Man, I love this place. I know I can come off as a jerk sometimes, but I love this city and this museum. I loved the expedition, too—until Henry was killed. But I can't let all our work fall apart, Harley. It meant too much to Henry. And it's too important for future generations."

"You're right," Harley agreed. "The cops—"

"Are idiots. Whoops, sorry. Maybe the Feds are better."

"Killers make mistakes—and they get caught," Harley said.

"And sometimes they don't."

"This time, they will."

"You haven't seen the half of it. The stuff here, Harley, it's ironic that it all started with a murder, isn't it? Amenmose, I mean. Maybe you can figure out who killed the guy. That was the major thing for you on our expedition, right?"

"Yep. I still find it incredibly interesting that he was killed, and yet he was rewarded with the kind of tomb that would allow him to move into the afterlife," Harley said.

"Come in today! I'll meet you at the doors. You'll be safe. Lots of cops around. I'll get you any piece of research material you want that I can find! I'll be like your apprentice!" Jensen said.

"Okay," Harley agreed. "I'll text you when I'm at the entrance."

She ended the call and glanced around the room, running her hands over the sheets. So much for luxuriating in memory.

She hurriedly showered and ran out, anxious to get to the subway and up to the museum.

Despite herself, she found that she kept scrutinizing the crowds of people who thronged around her. It was still morning rush hour. People were everywhere, on their way to work and school.

She was looking for a mummy, she realized.

That was ridiculous, she thought. And yesterday, it didn't seem bizarre at all that there'd be a mummy around; a mummy fit right in with the zombies.

Rush hour on Monday. Not likely that a mummy would be running around. Then again, it was New York, and people might see a mummy and merely shrug.

No mummies appeared—and she had to admit she was grateful.

As she neared the museum, she texted Jensen. He texted back that he'd meet her at the entrance.

Jensen and an NYPD officer were at the door; Jensen explained who she was and Harley showed the officer her ID.

She was allowed to come in.

It felt strange to walk through the entry with Jensen when everything was so empty. He told her there were at least ten police officers in the building, along with what he believed were "fledgling" FBI agents—probably bored to tears, but assigned to watch over the museum. Jensen talked about the museum itself with great enthusiasm; he just couldn't resist. She already knew that the facility was devoted to ancient civilizations, from Mesopotamia to Rome to Greece and ancient Egypt and other societies. He explained that he considered it a homage to humanity creating civilization; there was even a wonderful new section on the development of humans, back to the hominidae or great apes speciating from the ancestors of the lesser apes. "When this is…when this is solved, when things are back to normal, when life at least *feels* normal, you really have to come and spend a day here, just touring around, checking out the exhibits. It's a phenomenal museum. And I'm so happy to be here, except now the rest of the scientists, curators, historians—and even the café and gift shop employees!—hate us."

"Oh, I doubt that."

"Nope. It's true."

"When life does get back to normal, they won't hate you. And, as we've noted before, I'll bet all the insanity's going to make the museum more popular than ever. It has a really wicked mystery story now," Harley reminded him.

"Well, anyway, let's head back. In one of the prep clean rooms, there are some papers Henry'd been working on. Plus, there are a number of mummies in the room—still in their coffins, for the most part, except for our 'screaming' mummy, the one we saw with Henry before he...died. Anyway, I have a meeting with the museum director in a few minutes."

"Gordon Vincent," Harley murmured.

Jensen nodded. He glanced her way and sighed. "Yeah. They don't know if Arlo's going to make it or not. If he does, I heard he's probably going to be arrested."

"He didn't do it," Harley said again.

"But—"

"I'm telling you. He was a victim. Like Vivian."

"Well, from your lips to God's ears, right? Anyway—and honestly, I wouldn't want something to come about this way—I believe I'm going to be promoted to curator director for the Amenmose exhibit."

"Oh. Wow," Harley murmured. "Congratulations. Well, I guess… I mean, I understand, no one would want things to work this way, but wasn't Arlo employed by Alchemy?"

"Yes, but he was being offered the permanent position here," Jensen said.

They walked by the temple and the exhibits that were usually open to the public, then went to the employee section of the museum and one of the rooms next to Arlo's lab.

"It's mainly artifacts," Jensen said. "But that desk has boxes of Henry's notes. No one could read his scribbled handwriting as well as you could. Maybe you'll find something. I'll come back as soon as the meeting's over and we can go to lunch. Not in the museum, I'm afraid, since everything is closed down today. But I'm sure we can think of someplace you'll like."

"How about the sandwich shop over on

Sixth?" Harley suggested. "It's a five-minute walk."

He gave her a thumbs-up and left. She listened as the door clicked shut.

This room didn't require "clean" suits, but it was climate controlled. Harley assumed it would be taken for granted that anyone in the room would have complete respect for ancient sarcophagi, bodies and other artifacts.

For a moment, she just looked around.

Many things were still crated. There were just so many artifacts that they were switched in and out of the display. Some of the sarcophagi—the magnificent, beautifully designed and painted outer coffins—had been unpacked. They'd withstood time and climate well, since they were made of hardwood and precious metals.

Shelves on the wall held numerous canopic jars; others were heaped with jewelry. One shelf contained dozens of statuettes and, carefully set in a corner of the room, was a pile of chariot wheels, the body of a chariot and a set of harnesses.

Another shelf held several mummified cats.

Yet another held weapons, some of them simple, having belonged to rank-and-file soldiers. There were maces, shields, daggers, swords, knives and more. Some were inlaid with precious jewels and gold.

They were worth a small fortune.

But to the best of Harley's knowledge, nothing had ever disappeared from the museum.

The motive for murder wasn't for treasure. So it seemed, anyway. Then why…?

She shook her head. It was like a puzzle, as Micah had said—with one crucial missing piece. But if you could find all the pieces and put them together, a picture would emerge.

A picture from the past? Perhaps. And what might that have to do with the present? Probably nothing at all. But then again, sometimes just turning one's mind to a different puzzle helped solve the one that was more pressing.

Harley examined the many offerings in the room that would eventually be catalogued and join other treasures on the museum floor. Then she moved to the cheap aluminum desk—with the cheap aluminum chair in front of it—that was piled high with cardboard boxes of Henry Tomlinson's observations and recordings. They ranged from his calculations as to where they would find the tomb, to his reactions the day they discovered it. If she knew Henry, the boxes were also stuffed with research papers and anything else he'd found or received that complemented his own work.

Harley sat down and began to read.

Surely, museum staff had at least scanned them before this.

But maybe they hadn't read everything. Maybe they hadn't known Henry.

Maybe they hadn't been determined to catch a killer.

NED AND VIVIAN RICHTER had a house—a Victorian manor in Brooklyn, in the Williamsburg area, not far from Pratt Institute.

"Swanky," Craig murmured, ringing the bell.

"It is nice," Micah agreed. "When I was around here several years ago on that special assignment I worked with you, this area was still kind of sketchy. Lots of drugs and crime—and 'swanky' places like this were usually turned into frat houses or apartment buildings with dozens of closet-size apartments."

"This area has come up in the world—and someone's put real money into this house. But Richter's been a CEO on expeditions with Alchemy. I guess he's earned plenty of bonuses and more through the years," Craig said.

"I guess so."

Craig rang the bell again.

"What do you want to bet a maid's going to answer?" Micah asked.

"I wouldn't bet against you!" Craig replied.

"Nothing wrong with being rich," Micah said. "I'd love to try it one day."

They were right; the door was opened by a pretty young woman in a maid's outfit that would've done any movie set proud.

"May I help you?" she asked. She had a strong accent, possibly Slavic.

They showed their badges.

"We need to see Mr. and Mrs. Richter, please," Micah told her.

The woman pursed her lips. "You are aware, sir, that Mrs. Richter is just out of the hospital," she said.

"Yes, we are aware. We plan to be brief," Craig assured her.

She led them into a parlor that looked like a furniture showroom. Micah wondered if anyone had ever been in the room before.

But they were only there a minute or two before Vivian Richter made an appearance. "Gentlemen. What can I do for you? I'm about to head into the museum. With everything that's been going on... Well, I keep thinking that maybe someone's out to sabotage the exhibit. I keep going over our books, our notes—and, of course, our artifacts. I'm saying 'our.' They aren't ours, as I'm sure you realize. Everything we discovered will be returned to Egypt. We're not thieves anymore. There was a time, though… Did you know that during the Victorian era, mummies were so plentiful they were often used as kindling? That's shocking, isn't it?"

"I think I've heard that somewhere," Micah said.

"Well, anyway…how can I help you? Would you like to come into the museum with me?"

"Actually, we'd like to know where you were yesterday, once you got out of the hospital, and if you were with your husband all day. We'd like to speak with him, too."

"Ned's already gone to the museum. But in answer to your question, he was with me all day. He's a devoted husband."

"When did he leave?" Micah asked. "This morning, I mean."

"A little while ago, I believe," Vivian said.

"You *believe*? You didn't actually see him?" Craig asked.

"I spent yesterday and this morning sleeping, resting. I know when my husband's with me. I can feel his presence. Are either of you married? No? You see, after years of marriage, you don't need to *see*, gentlemen—you *feel*. You're both still young. Wait until you've been married for years. You'll understand what I'm talking about."

Vivian Richter was dressed in an attractive, businesslike pantsuit; she looked very thin and a little flushed, but otherwise well.

"Agents, why exactly are you questioning me?" she said to them. "I'm a victim. And you can't possibly suspect Ned of any wrongdoing! The whole expedition rested on his shoulders. He wouldn't want anything to go wrong."

"Our apologies, but questioning is necessary, under the circumstances," Micah said.

"Part of the job," Craig added ruefully.

"Oh, please!" Vivian said. "Agent Fox, I heard that you saved my life! And you, Agent Frasier, have been hard at work on the case. I'm grateful to you both, although—due to my recent bout with near death—I haven't had much chance to socialize with law enforcement."

"Mrs. Richter, I can't take credit for saving your life. Anyone there would have dialed 911," Micah said. "We're just glad to see you looking so well."

"Yes! I thank God!" she said. "Great hospital staff, wonderful EMTs… I'm a very lucky woman. I understand I was poisoned with insecticide but apparently, according to the doctors, there's been an upsurge in problems of that kind because of the liquid nicotine used in electronic cigarettes. They hit me with activated charcoal, and they monitored me for seizures. I was lucky, so lucky. I hear Arlo may not fare as well, that he was exposed to a heavier dose of poison and that he was unconscious when he was found. But I also heard that the police believe Arlo was guilty. That he might've been the 'mummy' who attacked me. Who meant to kill me!" she ended in a whisper. "Arlo and I... We worked well together. I thought so anyway. I wonder if he was worried because I'm married to Ned. Maybe he was worried that would put me in a better position for a raise at Alchemy. And I realize that some people are convinced that Henry was killed... I never knew what to think. I mean, we had to run! There was death coming at us from the desert!"

"Of course," Micah said sympathetically. "So, you believe we'll find Ned at the museum now?"

"Yes. He should be there working."

"But he didn't actually tell you he was going in. And you didn't actually see him," Craig said.

"No, as I was telling you..."

"Yes. You felt him. When's the last time you *saw* him?" Micah asked.

"I, uh… Yesterday's a bit of a blur for me. We left the hospital and then—"

"He came to the hospital to get you," Micah inserted.

"I told you! He's a loving and devoted husband," Vivian said. "Yes! He came to get me. I'm going to call your superiors, gentlemen, if you suggest once more that he's anything less than a wonderful man."

"You still didn't answer the question," Craig pointed out.

"All right! I don't know what time he left this morning. I know he was going to the museum. And he knew, of course—" She suddenly stopped speaking.

"Yes?" Micah prompted.

"I knew he was going into the museum, and he knew I was coming in later today. With everything that went on, and cops, technicians, crime scene people everywhere… I need to see to the integrity of our entire exhibit—especially in light of what happened to Arlo!"

"We'll see that you get there safely, Mrs. Richter," Craig offered. "We have a company car, so we can drop you off at the museum. However, considering what you've been through, I recommend you contact one of the policemen on duty there today. I think you should be under protection."

"I'll make a call," Micah said.

"It's not necessary to request protection," Vivian said. "Honestly, I'll be fine. Now I know to watch out for people coming near me."

"I'll make a call," Micah repeated firmly.

Vivian smiled. "Thank you. It's so lovely that you're watching out for me."

"We'll wait here until you're ready," Micah said.

"Well, then…thank you! Excuse me. I'll be right with you."

She left the room. "You'll take her in?" Micah asked Craig.

"You're going to speak with the house-keeper?"

"Yep."

"You think she's an illegal?"

"Yes. Okay, right now I'll call Egan and get him to talk to whoever's in charge of guarding the museum. They need to keep an eye on Vivian and get eyes on Ned Richter, too. Then I'll come back here and talk to the housekeeper. Find out the last time she saw Ned Richter."

"Okay. I'll get her to the museum," Craig said. He hesitated. "Richter. I just don't see him as a player in this game. He's in big with Alchemy, but he's not a fanatic Egyptologist."

"Maybe, this time around, jealousy isn't the motive," Micah said.

"Then what the hell is?" Craig murmured.

Vivian reappeared, a heavy bag over her shoulder. Craig politely took it for her, and they exited the house.

Micah opened the passenger door of the agency sedan for Vivian. She looked at him, obviously a little confused. "I don't mind riding in the back."

"Ah, but we'd rather have you ride up front with my partner. He'll enjoy your company," Micah said.

"You're not coming?"

"I have some things to do," Micah said vaguely. "Don't forget, Mrs. Richter—I'll get a cop assigned to you. Stay safe and take care of yourself."

When he started to close the car door, she stopped him. "Agent Fox, don't be suspicious of my husband. I know I'm repeating myself, but he's a very kind man. People love him and that's why he's good at his job. He'd never hurt me."

"Stay with an officer, Mrs. Richter," he said, and he managed to close the door.

He glanced back up at the house.

He thought he saw the drapes move and, as soon as the black agency sedan with Craig and Vivian Richter turned the corner, he went back up the walk to the door.

The housekeeper was afraid; he was certain of that. Her immigration status was probably not legal, as he and Craig had guessed.

She might try to hide.

But he wouldn't leave.

And he knew that—whether it was face-to-face or through the door—she would listen to him when he threatened her.

He hated threatening people, especially a young woman like this, working hard to get into the country.

But he had to know the truth.

Because someone else could die.

Standing there on the steps, waiting, Micah realized that he was afraid for more than just an elusive *someone.*

He was afraid for Harley. She'd been on that expedition, she'd been determined to voice her suspicions. Harley was poking her nose into everything.

And Harley Frasier was among those who might be targeted by a mummy. A living mummy armed with deadly poison.

Chapter Nine

Harley lost track of time.

She'd known for years, ever since she was a teenager and saw Craig join the FBI, that she wanted to solve crimes. She hadn't wanted to run around the streets with a gun, although she'd been more than willing to partake in classes at a shooting range. What she loved was the puzzle part of crime-solving. She also loved the concept of profiling, and was extremely glad of her friendship with Kieran Finnegan and, through her, Dr. Fuller and Dr. Mira. They were giving and generous with their time, and they'd talked to her upon occasion about criminal profiling. She'd considered going through still more school and entering the field of profiling.

She'd been part of the Amenmose expedition because of her fascination with figuring out motives, clues, possibilities. The puzzle aspects of a crime.

Not that solving the murder of a mummy could help with a present-day case.

Still, solving what might be considered an *extremely* cold case was certainly a useful exercise.

That afternoon, in the room with the mummies and the artifacts and Henry Tomlinson's notes, she found herself even more fascinated with the crime—committed thousands of years ago—because, despite time and place, people were people.

She was familiar with Tutankhamen, but read more about him, including some material that was new to her. She read about Ay. There were numerous references to Amenmose, as well. He knew the stars; he could navigate by them. He knew the heavens and the earth.

And he knew about Ra, about the dishonor Tutankhamen's father had done the ancient gods.

She reviewed the facts about Tut and Akhenaten in Henry's notes and translations, as well as those prepared by other scholars. The discovery of Tutankhamen's tomb by Howard Carter in 1922 had opened their ancient lives to investigation, leading to years of speculating. Some of that speculation had proven to be true; Akhenaten had tried to create a monotheistic society, his one god being Ra, the sun god. When Tutankhamen came to the throne, his father's efforts had been completely erased. In fact, his father's reign had been erased from records, and his mummy had disappeared.

Among Henry's papers, Harley found a research document dated 2010, of which he was a coauthor. It was about the discovery, in a cache of royal mummies, of one who'd proven through DNA testing to be Akhenaten.

But in Tut's time, there must've been many people who still believed what Tut's father had believed. Perhaps there were people prepared to kill a man like Amenmose, a man so ready to help Tut and Ay obliterate his father. Or not. Most experts concluded that Ay had ordered the murder.

Then Harley came across the translation of a letter mentioning a woman named Skrit; more digging showed that she was Amenmose's wife.

Harley rose and walked around the room for a moment. Was one of the mummies there Skrit?

She saw nothing that would indicate such a thing.

Why wasn't the woman buried with him?

Of course, the tomb had been a secret. Had she, his loving wife, planned it, planned the burial? Amenmose had been murdered, but he'd been given all the correct funeral rites such a man would have required.

Frustrated, Harley sat back down. She began to read and research again, referring not just to the notes they had, but looking up entries online made by scholars through the ages.

She stopped looking for Amenmose. She started looking for Skrit.

And what she found was truly fascinating.

Micah knocked again.

He knew the housekeeper was in the house.

He'd been there for nearly ten minutes, and she had yet to answer the door.

But he knew she was in there. And that she was hovering close to the door.

"I just have a few questions," he said loudly. "If you don't care to answer them…well, I can have some people from Immigration come down here in a few minutes. I can call Homeland Security, too."

The door finally opened. The pretty housekeeper stepped back. Her eyes were huge and wet with tears she was trying not to shed.

Micah felt like a real jerk. "I'm sorry," he

told her. "I don't want to hurt you in any way. I just have to ask you a few questions. And I need you to answer me honestly."

She nodded, looking anxiously out at the street, then pulled him quickly inside.

"I am Valeria. Valeria Andreev. I don't want to go back, please. I want to be legal. Mr. Richter has said he will help me. He pays me well. He is a kind man."

"I don't want you to be sent back, either. You obviously want to be here, and you seem to know the language well."

"I want to be American."

"We can try to help you. But I need your help."

She nodded again, an earnest expression on her face.

"Did Mr. Richter go to the hospital to bring Mrs. Richter home yesterday?"

"Yes, that is true. It is not a lie."

"What time was that?"

"Close to noon."

"Okay, thank you. And then?"

"And then Mrs. Richter asked me for juice and some food, and told me that she would sleep, and she didn't want to be disturbed."

"And?"

"I did not see her again until this morning."

"Okay, thank you. And what about Mr.

Richter? Did he stay with her? Talk to her, take care of her and make sure she was all right?"

Valeria looked stricken. She didn't want to tell the truth.

"I saw him... I saw him bring her home."

"He went into her room?"

"Yes."

"But he didn't stay there."

Valeria bit her lower lip and shook her head unhappily.

"I don't think so. I think...they argued. I think she was angry with him. I heard their voices, and then I heard nothing, and I thought..."

"Yes?"

"I thought I heard the door slam."

"Did you see when Mr. Richter left today?"

Valeria shook her head. "No... I... I saw him yesterday. I didn't see him at all today. But, of course, that means nothing. I do not sit here and stare at the door, you know. I don't mean to be a—what do you say?—wiseass. But I don't know."

Micah smiled. "It's okay. I don't think you're trying to be a wiseass. What you do know is this—Mr. and Mrs. Richter fought. They came home from the hospital yesterday at about noon. You saw them both go to her room. You haven't seen Mr. Richter since—and you saw Mrs. Richter for the first time today when you went to get her for my associate and me?"

Valeria nodded, wide-eyed.

Micah handed her one of his cards. "If you need help, call me."

Her eyes brightened and she held the card close to her chest.

Micah headed out to the street. He saw a taxi and grabbed it, pulling out his cell phone as he did.

They were nearing the bridge when he got through to Craig.

"The maid didn't actually see either of the Richters after about noon yesterday," he told Craig. "Until she brought her to the door this morning."

"Interesting," Craig said. "Because Ned Richter isn't at the museum. I talked to the officer in charge. No one's seen him since yesterday, sometime in the afternoon. In fact, right around the time Arlo Hampton was found."

HARLEY JUMPED UP, determined to find Jensen. She was almost certain that she'd discovered the truth about Amenmose. She'd put well-known facts together with information from less well-known sources—and had come up with her theory.

She wondered if there was a way to prove what she believed she knew.

Not easy.

Because, of course, if the murderer was Ay or any other person with power, he or she wouldn't have performed the deed himself—or herself. He—or she—would have had lackeys.

But Harley was convinced her theory made sense. Perfect sense.

Amenmose had been killed. He'd been killed because he'd secretly been a far greater fan of Tutankhamen's father than he'd ever let on. Ay had probably known that Amenmose whispered in the boy king's ear. Amenmose had been skilled at playing the political game. He'd pretended to listen to every word that left Ay's mouth; he'd proclaimed himself a man of the future, not the past. But in his heart, he'd felt certain that Tut's father had been right. And because of that—because those closest to him had known and others might have suspected—anyone connected to him, related to him, or even just a friend or servant to him, might have been in danger.

She left the room and glanced quickly down

the hall. There was no one to be seen; not a police officer, not an employee, no one.

"Jensen?"

No answer.

"Jensen, where the hell are you?" she wondered aloud.

She hurried down the hall, past the lab. No one there, either. Of course, Arlo was the person who usually worked in the lab. And Arlo...

She hadn't heard that he was dead. Maybe he was still clinging to life, even if his poisoning had been worse than Vivian's. She hoped so.

Because she just didn't believe that he was guilty.

"Jensen!"

Past the lab, she made for her friend's office and knocked. Once again, no answer. She tried the door and it opened easily, but Jensen wasn't inside.

"Damn you," she grumbled. "Bring me in—and then disappear!"

Harley closed the door and tried the offices of Vivian Richter, Ned Richter, Arlo—even the museum director, Gordon Vincent's. No one was in any of them.

As she stood there, she again heard the terrible screech of a cat.

Just as she had heard when she'd been looking at the cat mummy.

Nothing mysterious about that, she told herself. There was obviously a cat somewhere in the museum. She'd meant to ask someone. It had probably been a stray, and a museum employee, unable to stand the sight of the poor creature begging in the street, had brought it in. That person must have fed it and kept it hidden here somewhere.

Poor thing; it deserved better.

"Where are you?" she murmured aloud. "Little creature, where are you? Where's Jensen? Where's anyone?"

She went back into the hallway, listening for the cat.

She heard it meow. She thought the sound was coming from the walls—or from beneath her.

She guessed the cat was down in one of the old tunnels, maybe in a section of the abandoned subway.

Harley remembered the day she and Micah had been with Arlo, and she hurried to the stairway that led below.

It was dark, of course.

She had her flashlight—of course.

She turned it on and walked carefully down

the steps, first to the basement, through rooms and rooms of storage, and then down another level.

To tunnels of nothing.

To darkness that led nowhere.

And then she heard it again. It wasn't a scream this time. It was a pathetic kind of mewling.

She hadn't even seen the cat yet, but she felt so bad for the little creature, which was obviously scared. It probably had no idea where it was, how to get out, how to find help or sustenance.

Maybe she could keep a cat. A cat would be a good companion.

She wondered if Micah liked cats.

She wondered if it mattered.

Harley knew she was definitely in lust and halfway in love, but she'd told herself it *was just temporary*, that she expected nothing. He was living and working in Washington, DC, and he'd go back there. He'd given her no hint, nothing to suggest Harley should go back with him.

And yet she couldn't accept the fact that he might walk away. They'd met and joined forces over Henry. They got along extremely well, but they were both determined and stubborn, and she didn't intend to forget that she wanted to pursue her career.

Everything had begun just a few days ago, and already she couldn't imagine her life without him in it.

She gave a little scream, startled when the cat let out another mew. The sound was very close.

"Kitty, kitty, where are you?" she called.

The pathetic squeaking began again.

"Where are you? Come on, kitty, kitty, kitty. I'll help you!"

She came around a corner and almost fell into a niche in the wall. She tried to steady herself and realized she was leaning on an old maintenance door.

It creaked open on very rusty hinges.

She heard the cat cry again, really loudly this time. She'd found it!

"Hey, there you are," she said. "Come on, little one. I'll take you somewhere safe and warm and get you something to eat."

What if Micah Fox was allergic to kittens? She'd never asked him about pets.

She'd never asked him about anything. She'd just fallen into something crazy, she'd wanted him so desperately.

She shone her light around again, seeking the cat.

"Hey, sweet thing, I'm going to find you," Harley said out loud.

And then she froze as her light fell on the crying kitten.

And on so much more...

"GET IN HERE. We've got Sanford Wiley, our man in Cairo, ready for a video chat in twenty minutes," Richard Egan told Micah. "He has some information."

"On Satima Mahmoud?" Micah asked.

"That's what I imagine," Egan replied.

Craig was doing the driving. He was a damned good driver, and as a New Yorker, he could maneuver the streets as few could.

Micah had a feeling that whatever Sanford Wiley had discovered, it was important to their case.

He put a call through to Harley, anxious to talk to her, to hear her voice.

She didn't answer.

Craig glanced over at him.

"She didn't say she was going out," Micah murmured. "Or, she might have said that she was going to be with Kieran."

"I wouldn't worry. Leave a message. If she's on the subway, she won't get it for a while."

"I'll bet she went to the museum. Jensen—that friend of hers—I think he keeps encouraging her to come in. I don't feel good about it, but I'm not sure why."

"At least Vivian Richter seemed fine. She seems to believe that Arlo tried to kill her and that he might've killed Henry Tomlinson."

"Yeah, well, I *don't* believe it, and I'm positive you don't, either. Also, I know damned well that Harley doesn't believe it. And Craig, what I've said before is true—Harley's had more classes of all kinds than we have. Yes, in a classroom. She doesn't have much practical experience, not really. But she's smart as a whip. If she says something is off, it is."

"I'll call Kieran. She'll track her down. How's that?"

"Thanks. Tell her we'll join the tracking party as soon as we're done with the video chat," Micah said.

"Will do."

"She's at work, though, isn't she?"

"She won't have a problem. Tell them it's an active case and the good doctors will be more than happy to send Kieran off—or get into it themselves!" Craig assured him. He spoke to the car phone; it dialed Kieran.

"Anything new?" she asked. "What's going on?"

"Can you find Harley?" Craig asked her.

"Sure. I know where she is."

"You do?"

"At the museum. I talked to her briefly when she was on her way there. Jensen asked her to come in. They're good friends, you know, and I think he's feeling pretty lost and alone in all this."

"Yeah, lost and alone," Micah murmured. "Can you get over there? I tried to reach her by phone. She didn't answer."

"I'll go right over," Kieran promised. "I'll find her, don't worry. And when I do, we'll give you a call."

Kieran said goodbye and hung up; Craig looked at Micah. "Feel better?"

"I wish I did."

"You don't like Jensen."

Micah shook his head. "But he was with Harley when Henry was killed, so…"

"Yep." Craig was quiet for a minute, and Micah knew what he was thinking.

"Two people could've been involved," he said quietly. "It's a question of which two. Do you think maybe Ned Richter? Would Richter actually have done that to his own wife?"

"They fight quite a bit, or so we've heard," Craig said. "Yolanda told us she heard them arguing, and the maid told you that they were fighting yesterday."

"Yes, but…wrapping someone in nicotine-soaked linen?"

"She was found immediately. So she survived," Craig said.

They reached the office. Leaving the car, they hurried through the ground-floor security check and up to Egan's office.

Egan was already engaged in the call with Sanford Wiley.

On the video screen, they could see that Wiley looked glum.

"Did you find her? Did you find Satima Mahmoud?" Micah asked.

"Yeah, we found her," Wiley said.

"But you didn't bring her in."

"She's dead," Wiley told them.

Micah had been standing. He sank into one of the chairs in the conference room. "Dead? Not…as a mummy?"

"As a mummy? No. Right now, they have some of her friends in custody. She was likely killed by a member of her 'group'—although exactly who that is, I don't know—or by an enemy of this group. That's just what we're being told. The situation's complicated, but from what we've gleaned so far, there was no real insurrection planned for the night Henry Tomlinson died. We know this because the Egyptian police are questioning someone they pulled in. Some kid who didn't want to spend his life in prison. He says they were contacted by Satima Mahmoud. She had money, a lot of money. She was willing to pay them to get a fake insurrection going. That's why it was such a pitiable show. No one really wanted to bear arms, go against anything—or get caught," Wiley explained.

"So we've been thinking in the right direction," Micah said. "It was all a diversion to keep the police or any other authorities from discovering what really happened to Henry Tomlinson."

"Yes, that's what we believe on this end," Wiley said. "Satima Mahmoud was found with a bullet in her back. We think it could've been fired by someone in a group with a different political view for the future—or, as I said, someone in her own group. Many people were arrested for taking part in the so-called uprising. Perhaps someone wanted revenge."

"Still hard to understand," Craig said. "The Amenmose find was worth a fortune."

"Yes, there were priceless objects. And, yes, they might have wanted them for their monetary value to support their cause, whatever that was. Thing is, the black market is hard to navigate these days. And if you're caught… not good. Cash—cold hard cash—is far better than even a priceless object. Someone gave Satima a lot of cold hard cash. At the moment, that's all I know. If we get anything else…"

"Thank you, Wiley," Micah said. "You've been a tremendous help. I'm sorry the woman is dead," he added.

Egan finished up with Wiley, and they cut off the chat.

"Cold hard cash? Someone with access to a lot of it?" Egan mused. "That's not your average grad student."

"There's Richter," Craig said. "Or…well, some grad students come from family money. That's how they manage to study forever and ever. We have background checks on everyone. I've skimmed all the files…"

"Morrow, Jensen Morrow. His father invented some kind of cleaning product. He's got money," Micah said. But it was true, too, that they'd just left the Richter house, which had to be worth millions.

Craig nodded. "Yeah. But to be fair, it *could* be Richter. He'd have the money. He was supposedly with his wife when everything was going on back in the Sahara. We know now that the two of them fight, although Vivian Richter swears that her husband is totally loving and good."

"But the maid said differently," Craig pointed out.

"The maid?" Egan asked.

Craig waved a hand in the air and said, "Sir, I think we may have to help that woman out when this is all over. She talked to Micah about Richter's whereabouts."

"Go and get Vivian Richter," Egan said. "Bring her in. I think it's time we had a conversation here in the office."

"On our way!" Micah said.

They hurried back to the street where the car was waiting.

As they drove, Micah tried Harley's number again.

"Still not answering," he muttered to Craig.

"We'll find her," Craig promised. "Don't forget," he said, "she's my cousin."

There was a grim set to Craig Frasier's mouth.

Micah was glad for it. That meant he wasn't alone; they were going to find Harley, and they'd damned well find her fast—and she'd be all right.

IT WAS RIDICULOUS, it was horrible, and it was like something out of a horror movie by a master of the genre.

Harley had found the cat.

And the cat was sitting on the head of a man.

The man was dead. It was Richter. Ned Richter.

She couldn't scream.

The last thing she *should* do was scream!

In fact, she was worried about having her flashlight on. But the whiff of gases or decay, some ghastly smell, that was coming to her made Harley think the man she was staring at had been dead for some time, probably at least twenty-four hours.

He hadn't been wrapped in linen. He probably hadn't died from any kind of poisoning.

Ned had been stabbed through the heart with an Egyptian dagger. He was shoved up against a wall; he'd probably died right there, she surmised, studying the pool of blood that surrounded him. Blood that had grown sticky.

He'd been killed yesterday. Either just before Arlo had succumbed to the linen wrappings and their nicotine, or just after.

If Arlo had tried to kill Ned Richter... Wait, that made no sense. Why stab Ned with an ancient Egyptian dagger, and then dress up in linen wrappings himself?

And who the hell had that been on the

street, the person shorter than Arlo who'd approached her, touched her with the poison?

"Harley? Harley, where are you?"

Jensen?

Jensen was calling her now.

Sure, Jensen was taller than the figure who'd come up to her. But what if he was working with someone? What if he'd gone with her that night in the desert just to throw suspicion off himself? He hadn't killed Henry Tomlinson; that would've been impossible. But he might have been in on it.

She forced herself to stay silent.

But to her great distress, the kitten took that moment to mew desperately for help once again—apparently deciding that help wasn't going to come from Harley.

"Kitty! Aw, here, kitty, kitty!" Jensen said. "Who the hell would be keeping a cat down here?" he asked himself.

He was coming in her direction.

He didn't sound like a killer.

To make matters even worse, Harley's phone began to ring.

It was on vibrate, but even vibrate sounded shockingly loud to her!

She saw that it was Micah, and that he'd called several times. The calls hadn't gone through. Suddenly, now—now!—they were.

She backed as close as she could against the wall. She almost let out an involuntary scream; she'd backed into the corpse. She was stepping in the sticky blood.

"Micah!" she whispered.

He was talking as she answered. She didn't think he'd hear her, and she didn't think he had any idea that she wasn't in a good situation.

"Harley, you're at the museum, right? Kieran's coming there to get you. Leave. Leave with her. Wiley, the agent in Cairo told us Satima Mahmoud's body was found. She was killed either by a rival political group or by her own friends, they don't really know. But here's what's important—there was no insurrection. It was staged to cover up Henry's murder. The killer could be Ned Richter or possibly Jensen Morrow," Micah said. "You need to get out of there—"

"It's not Ned Richter," she said in a hoarse whisper.

"How do you know?"

"I'm looking at him. He's dead. Dagger to the heart," Harley said.

"Where are you?"

"Subbasement, I think. Near the old subway station."

"What are you doing down there, Harley?

Never mind, never mind. We're on our way.
You need to get out!"

"Yes, but—"

"Get the hell out of there now! It could be
Jensen. Get out, Harley!"

"I can't!" she whispered.

"Why not?"

"Jensen is down here, coming right at me."

Chapter Ten

There were a number of hallways and tunnels, entrances and exits down here.

Harley knew that because Arlo had shown her and Micah around the basement and sub-basement levels. She had to think; she had to remember everything they'd learned that day. She needed to…

Find a way out.

The kitten was continuing to cry. He had jumped off the body of Ned Richter and was coming to Harley at last, trying to wrap around her ankles.

Harley swept up the kitten.

Poor little thing was sticky with blood; so was she.

Ned Richter's blood. Ned hadn't done any of this. He was innocent—and he was dead. It was almost as if they'd all been victims of a pharaoh's curse.

"Hey, kitty, kitty! Where are you?" Jensen called. "Harley? Damn it. Where are you, girl? Why haven't the police gotten these damned tunnels closed yet?" he muttered to himself. "Harley? Hey, anybody down here?"

He was coming closer and closer.

A weapon. She needed a weapon!

There was a dead man right next to her. A dead man with a dagger protruding from his chest.

She carefully put down the kitten and crept toward Ned to get the dagger.

It wouldn't move! It was stuck deep in his chest, as if the man's body, his flesh and blood and bone, refused to give up what had brought about its demise!

She would've sworn out loud except that Jensen was coming closer and closer.

Micah and Craig were on their way. They'd be here soon. Kieran was up in the museum somewhere, and it was crawling with police. Kieran wouldn't wait long when she couldn't find Harley; she'd insist that the police start searching the place, tearing it apart.

"Harley?"

Jensen couldn't be more than twenty or twenty-five feet from her.

"Jensen Morrow! Stop right where you are!" a male voice thundered.

Harley knew the voice—it was McGrady. Detective McGrady. He'd followed Jensen down here. She hadn't even seen him, hadn't known he was at the museum.

Harley switched off her penlight.

The darkness seemed overwhelming, except...

She could see Jensen. He had his own light. "McGrady, what the hell is the matter with you? I'm trying to find Harley. You can help me. Harley, where are you and what the hell... Jeez! What's that smell? Is it cat poop? If so, it's the worst damn cat poop I've ever smelled."

He was talking about cat poop. He didn't know he was smelling a dead man. But if he'd killed Ned Richter, he would know.

"Stop, Morrow, or I'll shoot you, you murdering bastard!" McGrady called out.

"What?" Jensen demanded, obviously thrown. "I stopped! I'm right here."

Harley straightened in the dark, letting out a breath. McGrady was here. He was a cop. He had a gun.

But Jensen wasn't guilty. He was just looking for her. Looking for a cat. She believed it with her whole heart.

Harley held her breath for a minute, afraid

to speak, to cry out—to warn Jensen and the cop—and afraid not to.

She had solved one mystery that afternoon. The mystery of Amenmose's death. His wife, Skrit, had ordered him killed. She had hired the assassins. She hadn't hated him—well, maybe she had. But despite wanting him dead, she hadn't wanted him deprived of an afterlife. She'd seen to it that he'd died; she had done so to protect herself and their children from the growing power of Ay. She'd been no threat to Ay's position, but her husband had. Still, she hadn't denied him their form of heaven.

And now...

"Harley!" Jensen called, sounding desperate.

She stepped into the darkness of the hall, ready to call his name.

But just as she did, she saw a dark figure streak out from behind Jensen, coming straight at him.

"Jensen! Watch out!"

Harley screamed the warning just in time. He spun around, avoiding a lethal blow from Vivian Richter, who was wielding a jewel-encrusted pike. But Vivian was quick to double back, hitting him hard on the head with the end of her weapon.

Jensen went down. And as he did, his light went out.

"What the hell?" McGrady roared. "Mrs. Richter, are you all right? Are you all right?"

Something flew through the tunnel—heading directly for the cop. Harley cried out his name. "McGrady! Get down!" she shrieked.

She couldn't see what happened next.

Jensen's light was gone; McGrady's was, too.

Harley and Vivian Richter were both suddenly left in absolute, subterranean darkness.

CRAIG AND MICAH arrived at the museum just in time to find Kieran telling a policeman that she was going down to the basement, with or without him, but if he valued his employment, he would be accompanying her.

The policeman was telling her that an officer had already gone down, following Jensen Morrow.

"Detective McGrady is down there. He said there's no good reason for any of those science people to be running around in the basement."

Micah didn't wait; he had to get down to the subterranean levels.

Craig went to explain to the officer that they were FBI and to get Kieran, from where she had been speaking with the cop.

Micah ran, ran hard. He reached the stairs Arlo Hampton had so recently shown him. He stumbled down them, afraid to use his penlight.

When he got to the bottom, he paused.

He began to move slowly, feeling his way.

Then he smelled death.

Yes, as Harley had told him, Ned Richter was down here. And he was dead.

Had Jensen Morrow killed him?

"Help! Oh, my God, help me!"

He heard the cry. It came from ahead, down the long hallway before him. It was coming, he thought, from the abandoned subway section where they'd found the stash of insecticide. The nicotine poison.

The voice belonged to Vivian Richter.

"I'm coming!" he called. "Are you okay? Are you in distress?"

"No…he's going to kill me. Agent Fox? It's Jensen. He's going to kill me. He and Arlo… they killed Henry. The two of them. They tried to kill me. Jensen tried to kill Arlo because he had to make it look like Arlo had worked alone… Oh, my God! He killed my husband. Jensen killed Ned, my poor Ned!"

"Where are you?" Micah asked.

He was moving very slowly and very carefully, determined not to give away his position. But as he spoke, he ran into something with his foot.

Something hard—and soft at the same time.

He stooped down, his heart in his throat. A body.

Harley?

It wasn't Harley. He quickly realized it was a man.

Ned Richter? Jensen Morrow?

It couldn't be Ned Richter; he wouldn't be warm.

He wouldn't be…breathing.

"So that's it!" he said loudly, checking for Jensen's pulse. It was weak, but it was there. The man would need help, though, and fast.

"Vivian, where are you? You poor woman, attacked… Thank God Arlo was still so new at it. He ended up killing himself, but you're all right, barely touched! And Ned—killed by Jensen! Where are you? Let me help."

They were both playing a game, pretending they believed what the other claimed as truth.

Harley. Where the hell was Harley? Was the woman holding her somewhere? Was she down on the ground, dying…bleeding?

He heard a scream of rage.

Light suddenly filled the dank, dark space. And he saw Vivian. She was bursting out of the old subway tunnel, a lantern in one hand, a dagger held high in the other.

She was coming right at him.

He stepped out of the way; she would catapult into the wall.

But she didn't.

Because there was another cry of rage that tore through the darkness and death and decay of the tunnel.

It was Harley. And she'd found a weapon of her own—an old paving brick. She flew at Vivian, encountering her before Vivian could close in on Micah.

Both women went flying down to the floor. Vivian's lantern rolled away as they fell, casting light and shadow everywhere.

Micah reached down, catching Vivian's arm, grasping it hard.

Vivian screamed and released the antique dagger from the painful pressure he'd placed on her arm. He kicked it far from her.

Footsteps pounded down the length of the tunnel hall. Craig was there, Kieran right behind him.

Micah walked away from Vivian and drew Harley to her feet and into his arms. He held her; he wanted to hold her forever in the strange darkness and shadows, keep her from the horrors.

But of course, he couldn't.

Time meant everything just now.

"We need an ambulance for Jensen," he said. "And…"

"McGrady's here, too. I don't know how badly he's hurt. He's here somewhere!"

"Here! Here I am!"

They saw a form stumble toward them. And as it did, the tunnel blazed with light. Police officers, all carrying lights, came surging toward them.

"It was her!" McGrady said, swallowing hard, shaking his head. "Her! The woman poisoned herself to throw off any suspicion. She killed Henry, and she killed her husband. Yeah?"

Craig had Vivian Richter up by then. She was in handcuffs—and spitting mad. "I shouldn't have had to kill the bastard! Don't you get it? That mealymouthed little snake, Arlo Hampton—he was supposed to kill Ned. I did away with Henry Tomlinson, and Arlo was supposed to kill Ned. He said he couldn't do it! But I got him…oh yeah, I got both of them!"

"Who the hell would have suspected this!" McGrady said.

Micah looked at Harley, and his eyes darkened with concern.

"There's blood on you!" he murmured.

"Not mine," Harley said.

"Thank God." Micah looked toward Mc-Grady. "Then we're ready for the next step."

Harley smiled and nodded.

"McGrady, go ahead, do the honors. Bring Mrs. Richter in. We'll handle things down here. We'll get the medical examiner and the techs for Mr. Richter," Micah said.

"And an ambulance for Jensen. She got him pretty good," Harley said.

"Why don't you and Kieran go to the hospital with him?" Micah suggested.

"Yeah. Yeah."

They stared at each other for another long moment.

Then Harley turned away, bending down to Jensen. The EMTs arrived, followed by the medical examiner and the crime scene people.

And the night went on.

LIGHT CONTINUED TO blaze through the tunnels and the abandoned subway station as day turned to night, as the medical examiner came, as the body of Ned Richter was taken at last to the morgue.

Micah and Craig worked the tie-up in the tunnels. Long hours, a lot of waiting, a lot of speculating and figuring.

Meanwhile, Vivian had been questioned at the station—and confessed to everything, despite her attorney's cautions.

"The whole thing sounds like Hitchcock," Micah told Craig. "In a sick and twisted way. *Strangers on a Train*, except they weren't strangers. Vivian Richter was working with Arlo Hampton. Arlo wanted Henry's place as lead of the expedition. And Vivian was willing to kill Henry. It was an easy trade, or so it seemed. She'd kill Henry and Arlo would kill Ned. And, of course, she was willing to pay so that Satima Mahmoud would get her political group of disenfranchised students to fake an insurgency to cover up the murder. But as I said, in return for Henry being killed, Arlo was supposed to kill Ned. He screwed up. Vivian was afraid that Joe Rosello might figure out that Satima Mahmoud had been paid, so she decided she should poison him, which was why she showed up at the parade. And it was how Harley knew it wasn't the same mummy. Vivian is nowhere near as tall as Arlo. But Arlo didn't follow through on his part of the bargain. And Vivian lost control. When she saw Harley, I guess she wanted to do her in. But she hated Arlo for leaving her in the lurch. She was ready to kill Ned without blinking—and poison Arlo."

"Yeah, so all that 'beloved husband' stuff was just an act. For our benefit," Craig muttered.

"In Vivian's mind, her husband never gave her the respect she deserved. She was bitter, says he constantly claimed that she only had a job because of him. I guess she grew to hate him. If Arlo had played his part properly, he would've been the big cheese and she would've held the second position. But Arlo failed her, so she poisoned him. Otherwise, what was he going to do? Blame her."

"So if Arlo does make it, he'll be under arrest. Conspiracy to commit murder—even if he chickened out on it," Craig said.

"Yeah," Micah agreed. "But…"

"But?"

"I'm glad that Jensen Morrow and the other grad students have been proven innocent. They're Harley's friends. For her, I'm happy."

"Yep. I'm going topside for a while. I'll try to find out about Jensen's condition," Craig told Micah. "I'll let you know."

Micah nodded. He hoped Jensen Morrow was going to be okay.

He was, Craig reported a short time later, upon returning to the tunnels. Jensen had a concussion, and they'd watch him at the hospital for a few days. After that, he'd be as good as new, according to the doctors.

Finally, just as dawn was breaking, they finished in the tunnels.

He and Craig left.

Craig didn't ask where he wanted to go. He dropped him off at Harley's.

"I should've called her, I guess," Micah said.

"She'll be waiting for you," Craig told him.

And she was.

The night security guard waved him in. He had no idea how Harley knew exactly when he'd reach her door, but somehow she did.

The door opened, and she hurried into his arms.

He held her tight. She was bathed and sweet and fresh, and the scent of her hair was intoxicating; he kissed her, a long and lovely kiss, then pulled away.

"The tunnels," he said with a shudder.

And the blood of a dead man and the rot of millennia, he might have said.

He didn't need to.

She drew him in and up the stairs, to the bedroom, where he tossed his gun and holster on the table, and undressed quickly with her help. In minutes, she got into the shower behind him, forgetting to shed whatever silky thing she was wearing.

The water was hot and wonderful. Sensual, erotic and yet comforting.

He wasn't sure when they left the shower; he wasn't sure when she shed the wet silky thing. He knew they were still damp when they fell onto her bed. The room was in shadows, dawn was breaking with a spectacular light, and nothing seemed to matter except that they were together, touching each other.

They licked, teased, breathed each other.

Made love.

And made love again.

And then they slept for hours and hours and finally awoke.

Just for good measure, they made love yet again.

Later, when another day was almost gone, Micah looked through the great windows at the beauty of the church beyond.

"We're going to get married there," he said.

And then, of course, he remembered that they'd really only known each other for less than a week.

"One day," he added. "Somewhere along the line."

"What a proposal," she said lightly. "So romantic!" But she smiled. "One day... Yes, I like it. I like it very much!"

As she replied, he suddenly heard a mewling sound. He looked at her with surprise.

"Oh!" she murmured.

She hurried away and returned with a little ball of gray fluff in her arms.

"Um, we have a kitten. I hope that's okay?"

He laughed. "How did you...?"

"I found him in the tunnel. With... Ned's body. I think he helped us, really. He...he needs a home."

"So where has the little guy been?"

"I guess he went into hiding while we were all down there."

"And then?"

"He followed me up to the ground floor, and one of the officers took him for me until I got back from seeing Jensen at the hospital," she said. "I was thinking of calling him Lucky."

"Lucky it is," he said, and he took her—and the ball of fluff—back into his arms.

Lucky.

Yes.

Epilogue

"I was part of it all—and I still don't get it," Jensen said, shaking his head. "Okay, back to the beginning. Vivian Richter and Arlo Hampton made some kind of devil's bargain. She'd kill Henry. He'd kill Ned. And no one would suspect either of them because it wouldn't make sense. They wouldn't be guilty of the same crime. But Micah wasn't going to give up and they both knew he was coming to the opening of the exhibit. So she poisoned herself to throw off any possible suspicion?"

"Something like that," Harley said. She'd just finished up the last of the work she'd told Jensen she would do. With Arlo and Vivian gone, he'd fallen behind with the exhibit. She'd also been eager to finish what she'd written about the murder of Amenmose. Everything would be on record at the museum, but it was a museum specializing in the ancient world—and her job here had been to explain what had happened to Amenmose and how it had all fit in with that world.

For Henry.

Arlo was still in the hospital. He'd regained consciousness, but the poison had swept away a great deal of his mind.

He had no idea he was guilty of conspiracy. Sadly, he wasn't even sure who he was anymore, or what he'd done.

Vivian's attorney was still telling her to shut up. She, too, however, had apparently had some kind of mental breakdown, because she wouldn't stop talking to the press. She was going to go for an affirmative defense and claim that she'd been horribly abused by her husband and that he'd made her say things that weren't true. She also insisted that Henry Tomlinson had killed himself and that she'd long been a victim of chauvinism and abuse at the hands of both men.

"It's crazy. All crazy, huh?" Jensen asked her. "And you know what's even crazier? That horrible woman killed Henry and her husband, she tried to kill you and me and that cop—and I still love being at the museum."

"It's a good museum. Henry was a very special man, and loving the museum just honors him," Harley said.

"Hmm. And what about that cop? He was a jerk, and…well, you know, he came by to apologize to me."

"McGrady," Harley said. "Yep. He apologized to me, too. And thanked me for saving his life. He told me he's going to be a good cop—and that it'll be because of me! I sure hope that's true."

"You can find out, I guess."

Harley smiled. "Not for a while," she said softly. "For right now—"

She stopped talking and got up; she saw that Micah and Craig had come into Finnegan's. She waved, so the two of them could see her.

"Still don't see why you have to go to Washington," Jensen said.

Harley flashed him a smile. "Because I'm in love," she told him.

"Yeah, yeah. And okay, he's decent. And I'm happy for you both."

"Funny, he says you're decent, too. And he's happy we're friends."

By then, Micah had come to the table. He greeted her with a kiss and Jensen with a handshake.

Craig reached the table next, and then Kieran arrived from her day job. Kevin came over, then Kieran's youngest brother, Danny, and her older brother, Declan, joined them. Micah and Harley were surrounded by friends and family, and they were toasted. It was something of a goodbye party.

They might come back to New York eventually; a transfer was always possible for Micah. But Harley wanted to train with the FBI academy and work toward joining a profiling team.

Washington was best for both of them right now. Harley wasn't giving up her uncle's apartment; they'd be up visiting often enough.

Everyone talked; everyone had a great time.

Joe, Roger and Belinda came later—with Belinda being the happiest of the bunch. Her fiancé was back from his deployment overseas and their wedding was coming up.

"Will there be any kind of Egyptian motif?" Joe asked Belinda, smiling.

"No!"

"What about you guys?" Jensen asked Harley.

"No! Grace Church, and you're all invited. We'll let you know when."

"No zombies, mummies, or any form of ancient lore?" Joe asked.

"No!" Harley and Micah said together, the word emphatic.

They celebrated awhile longer. Then it was time to split up, and they hugged and kissed each other on the cheek and promised to stay in touch.

The most difficult thing for Harley was to say goodbye to Kieran and Craig, but they wouldn't be far away and they'd all go back and forth often.

"I know you don't have a firm date for the wedding yet, but what are you thinking?" Kieran asked Harley.

"We have no solid plans yet. We just know where," she said. "What about you two?"

Kieran laughed. "We have no solid plans, either. Not yet. All we know is that we *will* have a wedding, and oh, yes! The reception will be here!"

Micah caught Harley's hand. "We have a lot of dating to do," he told Kieran and Craig. "And apparently my proposal was lacking. I'm going to work on a better one. I'll fill you in on how that goes. We might take a honeymoon before we actually do the marriage thing. I want to make sure Harley knows we have some great history down Virginia way, too. It's not ancient, but it's pretty cool. I've got a friend who's working a dig in Jamestown. We can visit him for a while. And meanwhile, we'll date…"

They left. They went to spend their last night in the apartment with the great windows and the beautiful loft that they'd have for a while.

"Yes, we need to date…" Micah said.

Harley whispered in his ear.

He smiled. "Oh yeah. That, too. Lots and lots of that!"

The moon shone through the windows.

They hurried up the curving wrought iron stairway.

Tonight was an ending and a beginning.

And a beautiful night, made for love and for loving.

* * * * *

Get 2 Free Books,
Plus 2 Free Gifts—
just for trying the Reader Service!

HARLEQUIN *superromance*

HSRLP17R